W9-ADL-924

LOUIS B. WRIGHT, General Editor. Director of the Folger Shakespeare Library from 1948 until his retirement in 1968, Dr. Wright has devoted over forty years to the study of the Shakespearean period. In 1926 he completed his doctoral thesis on "Vaudeville Elements in Elizabethan Drama" and subsequently published many articles on the stagecraft and theatre of Shakespeare's day. He is the author of *Middle-Class Culture in Elizabethan England* (1935), *Religion and Empire* (1942), *The Elizabethans' America* (1965), and many other books and essays on the history and literature of the Tudor and Stuart periods, including *Shakespeare for Everyman* (1964). Dr. Wright has taught at the universities of North Carolina, California at Los Angeles, Michigan, Minnesota, and other American institutions. From 1932 to 1948 he was instrumental in developing the research program of the Henry E. Huntington Library and Art Gallery. During his tenure as Director, the Folger Shakespeare Library became one of the leading research institutions of the world for the study of the backgrounds of Anglo-American civilization.

VIRGINIA A. LaMAR, Assistant Editor. A member of the staff of the Folger Shakespeare Library from 1946 until her death in 1968, Miss LaMar served as research assistant to the Director and as Executive Secretary. Prior to 1946 Miss LaMar had been a secretary in the British Admiralty Delegation in Washington, D.C., receiving the King's Medal in 1945 for her services. She was coeditor of the *Historie of Travell into Virginia Britania* by William Strachey, published by The Hakluyt Society in 1953, and author of *English Dress in the Age of Shakespeare* and *Travel and Roads in England* in the "Folger Booklets on Tudor and Stuart Civilization" series.

The Folger Shakespeare Library

The Folger Shakespeare Library in Washington, D.C., a research institute founded and endowed by Henry Clay Folger and administered by the Trustees of Amherst College, contains the world's largest collection of Shakespeareana. Although the Folger Library's primary purpose is to encourage advanced research in history and literature, it has continually exhibited a profound concern in stimulating a popular interest in the Elizabethan period.

THE SECOND PART OF HENRY THE SIXTH

By

WILLIAM SHAKESPEARE

WASHINGTON SQUARE PRESS
PUBLISHED BY POCKET BOOKS
New York London Toronto Sydney Tokyo

Front cover courtesy of SHM28534 Henry VI of England (1421-71) by Francois Clouet (c.1510-72) (school of) Manor House, Stanton Harcourt, Oxon./Bridgeman Art Library, London

WSP

A Washington Square Press publication of
POCKET BOOKS, a division of Simon & Schuster Inc.
1230 Avenue of the Americas, New York, N.Y. 10020

Copyright © 1966 by Simon & Schuster Inc.

ISBN: 0-671-66919-2

First Washington Square Press printing February 1967

13 12 11 10 9 8 7 6 5

WASHINGTON SQUARE PRESS and WSP colophon are
registered trademarks of Simon & Schuster Inc.

Printed in the U.S.A.

Preface

This edition of *The Second Part of Henry VI* is designed to make available a readable text of Shakespeare's treatment of one segment of the troubled reign of Henry VI, the last Lancastrian King of England. In the centuries since Shakespeare, many changes have occurred in the meanings of words, and some clarification of Shakespeare's vocabulary may be helpful. To provide the reader with necessary notes in the most accessible format, we have placed them on the pages facing the text that they explain. We have tried to make them as brief and simple as possible. Preliminary to the text we have also included a brief statement of essential information about Shakespeare and his stage. Readers desiring more detailed information should refer to the books suggested in the references, and if still further information is needed, the bibliographies in those books will provide the necessary clues to the literature of the subject.

The early texts of Shakespeare's plays provide only scattered stage directions and no indications of setting, and it is conventional for modern editors to add these to clarify the action. Such additions, and additions to entrances and exits, as well as many indications of act and scene divisions, are placed in square brackets.

All illustrations are from material in the Folger Library collections.

L. B. W.
V. A. L.

March 15, 1966

Forecast of Genius

The Second Part of Henry VI is believed by most modern scholars to be the first portion composed by Shakespeare of the saga of Henry VI's unhappy reign. Although earlier scholars thought that Shakespeare had collaborators in the composition of the play (perhaps Greene, Nash, or Peele), more recent opinion leans to the view that Shakespeare was the sole author. *Henry VI, Part 2* clearly shows elements of the genius that Shakespeare was later to display in character portrayal as well as in a sense of theatrical effectiveness in his selection of details for stage representation. There is no good reason to doubt his authorship of the entire play.

In *Henry VI, Part 2*, the author is concerned with the problem of civil war and the disasters that such conflicts bring upon the state. This was a theme certain to attract attention and hold the interest of an Elizabethan audience. The Wars of the Roses, which *Henry VI* brings to the stage, had ended with the accession of the founder of the Tudor dynasty, Henry VII, and every literate person of Shakespeare's day had read some account of these events in the various chronicle histories then available. Furthermore, Elizabethans were profoundly interested in the theme, for lurking in the backs of their minds was the fearful thought that on the death of their queen, who had no direct heir, civil war might return to plague them. Everyone was fearful of civil disturbance. Everyone looked to the future with some misgivings. When an Elizabethan went to the parish church, he might hear read a sermon from the *Book of Homilies* on the heinous sin of rebellion. The compilers of this volume of official sermons, designed to be read in all parish churches, had been careful to include two on the wickedness of rebellion and civil strife.

Other writers besides Shakespeare found the wars that racked England through much of the fifteenth century favorite themes for both prose and poetry. The authors of English chronicle histories stressed the civil wars. The chronicler who gave greatest emphasis to these conflicts was Edward Hall (or Halle), who first published in 1542 a history called *The Union of the Two Noble and Illustrious Families of Lancaster and York*. This work appeared with slightly variant titles in at least four later editions and was used by Raphael Holinshed in the compilation of *The Chronicles of England, Scotland, and Ireland* (1577; later reprinted in 1587). Shakespeare drew on both Hall and Holinshed in *Henry VI, Part 2*.

In the selection of historical episodes, Shakespeare made free with history when dramatic requirements necessitated some alteration in the facts. For example, for some of the Jack Cade scenes, the author went back to a rebellion some seventy years before, that of Wat Tyler. He also utilized a quarrel scene between Queen Margaret and the Duchess of Gloucester which is not confirmed by history, for the

Title page of Holinshed's *Chronicles*, the major source for Shakespeare's history plays.

Duchess' disgrace and banishment from the court
occurred before Margaret married King Henry. The
emphasis on Margaret's love for the Duke of Suffolk,
which makes good theatre, is also not historically
justified.

But Shakespeare was a dramatist and not a
chronicler, and he felt free to employ poetic license
to heighten his dramatic effects.

In *The Second Part of Henry VI*, one can discern
qualities that would distinguish Shakespeare's later
and more fully developed plays. For example, he
is already interested in character and studies in the
contrast of characters. The figures who cross the
stage in *Henry VI, Part 2* are something more than
abstractions or mere names from the chronicles. In
the interpretation of Queen Margaret we see a
precursor of Lady Macbeth; a woman with a soul
of iron, she is determined to rule or ruin. Although
the Duke of York is portrayed as the conventional
Machiavellian of overweening ambition, a type of
character popularized on the stage by Marlowe and
others, Shakespeare gives him human qualities that
make him stand out as an individual rather than as
an abstract type. York's son, Richard (later Richard
III), already foreshadows the evil genius that Shakespeare was to give him in the play that bears his
name. Warwick, Clifford, Suffolk, and others are
also individuals whom one can remember, not merely as names, but as living beings.

Perhaps the most significant foreshadowing of
Shakespeare's later genius comes in the portrayal of
Jack Cade and his followers, the "rude mechanicals,"

Henry VI. From John Speed, *The Theatre of the Empire of Great Britain* (1627).

akin to many who were to appear in the later plays. Cade himself is distinctly drawn, a rabble-rouser who appears in scenes of macabre humor which hold the audience's interest. The Cade scenes, which make up most of Act IV, were carefully written to provide a contrast in character and atmosphere with the scenes of conflict between the opposing knights of York and Lancaster. Although death stalks the Cade scenes, the effect is that of grim humor, and Elizabethan audiences found much to laugh at in the interpretation of Cade and his henchmen. They would laugh at the weaver, the butcher, and others of Cade's crew as they would later laugh at Falstaff's companions in the Boar's Head Tavern or at the mechanicals in *A Midsummer Night's Dream*. Shakespeare, who delighted in portraying countrymen and artisans, made a significant beginning in *Henry VI, Part 2*.

The Cade scenes, however, have a deeper significance. In them, Shakespeare reveals his own disdain of the mob and his conception of the fickleness of the ignorant multitude who can be swayed by any demagogue. This belief he was later to exemplify in *Julius Caesar*, in *Coriolanus*, and in other plays. Like most of his contemporaries, Shakespeare had no sentimental notions about the essential goodness of mankind. The mob was easily moved by any clever rogue; it was fickle and changeable as the wind; and it was a potential danger to the state unless a strong government held it in subjection. That was the lesson that the Jack Cade scenes taught.

Edward III. From John Taylor, *All the Works* (1630).

In _The First Part of Henry VI_, the dramatist emphasizes the loss of the French provinces and the shame which that loss brought to the realm. Much of the action takes place in France, and we see the beginning of the civil strife that becomes the central theme of the two later plays on King Henry VI. Part 2 draws the lines of struggle between the houses of York and Lancaster more clearly. In this play, Shakespeare begins the battles that were to determine the fates of many of the leading participants. Part 2 ends abruptly with the Battle of St. Albans, which leaves the Yorkists in possession of the field. King Henry, however, has escaped, and his forces are on the way to London, where they propose to call a meeting of Parliament. Here Part 2 leaves the spectator or reader wondering how the sequel will present the succeeding events.

Part 2 does not fit the nineteenth-century notion of the "well-made play." It is merely a string of historical episodes, some of which are only loosely connected. The incidents involving Jack Cade, for example, have little to do with the main actions concerned with the conflict between the Yorkists and Lancastrians. Nevertheless, the Cade episodes foreshadow Shakespeare's use of a subplot in _Henry IV_ and _Henry V_, in which the scenes of low life do have an integral connection with the main plot. _Henry VI_ is the work of an apprentice in the theatre, but the three parts of this play already indicate the genius that was to flower in the later histories.

The present text of _Henry VI, Part 2_ is based on the Folio version printed in 1623. The quarto version, printed in 1594 with the title *The First Part of the Contention betwixt the Two Famous Houses of York and Lancaster*, is now regarded as a corrupt text of Part 2, probably put together by one or more actors from memory. A quarto play published in 1595 with the title *The True Tragedy of Richard Duke of York and the Death of Good King Henry the Sixth* is now generally accepted as a corrupt version of *Henry VI, Part 3*. Formerly, scholars maintained that these two quartos represented old plays that Shakespeare, perhaps with the help of others, revised to make Parts 2 and 3 of *Henry VI*. Recent studies, particularly the work of Professors Peter Alexander, Madeleine Doran, and Andrew S. Cairncross, demonstrate that the quartos are derived from Shakespeare's plays rather than the reverse.

The text printed in the Folio contains many errors which require emendation. Indications point to the use of a playhouse manuscript as printer's copy, and some evidence also suggests that the editors of the First Folio may have consulted the bad quartos in trying to straighten out passages that may have been illegible in their copy.

Henry VI, Part 2 was probably first acted in the season of 1590–91 and apparently met with success. Records of later performances are scanty. Edmund Kean in 1817 acted in a play called *Richard Duke of York* that was patched together from all three parts of *Henry VI*. Part 2 was performed in London in 1864, and all three parts of the play were acted at Stratford-upon-Avon in 1906. Since then, the play has been revived from time to time in aca-

demic and little theatres. The most notable recent
performances were those put on at Stratford-upon-
Avon by the Royal Shakespeare Company in 1963–
64, in a series of history plays called collectively
"The Wars of the Roses." The three parts of *Henry
VI* were condensed into two plays, the second of
which appeared under the title *Edward IV*. The
plays have been condensed still further for recent
television performance.

THE AUTHOR

As early as 1598 Shakespeare was so well known as
a literary and dramatic craftsman that Francis
Meres, in his *Palladis Tamia: Wits Treasury*, referred in flattering terms to him as "mellifluous and
honey-tongued Shakespeare," famous for his *Venus
and Adonis*, his *Lucrece*, and "his sugared sonnets,"
which were circulating "among his private friends."
Meres observes further that "as Plautus and Seneca
are accounted the best for comedy and tragedy
among the Latins, so Shakespeare among the English is the most excellent in both kinds for the
stage," and he mentions a dozen plays that had
made a name for Shakespeare. He concludes with
the remark that "the Muses would speak with
Shakespeare's fine filed phrase if they would speak
English."

To those acquainted with the history of the Elizabethan and Jacobean periods, it is incredible that
anyone should be so naïve or ignorant as to doubt

the reality of Shakespeare as the author of the plays that bear his name. Yet so much nonsense has been written about other "candidates" for the plays that it is well to remind readers that no credible evidence that would stand up in a court of law has ever been adduced to prove either that Shakespeare did not write his plays or that anyone else wrote them. All the theories offered for the authorship of Francis Bacon, the Earl of Derby, the Earl of Oxford, the Earl of Hertford, Christopher Marlowe, and a score of other candidates are mere conjectures spun from the active imaginations of persons who confuse hypothesis and conjecture with evidence.

As Meres's statement of 1598 indicates, Shakespeare was already a popular playwright whose name carried weight at the box office. The obvious reputation of Shakespeare as early as 1598 makes the effort to prove him a myth one of the most absurd in the history of human perversity.

The anti-Shakespeareans talk darkly about a plot of vested interests to maintain the authorship of Shakespeare. Nobody has any vested interest in Shakespeare, but every scholar is interested in the truth and in the quality of evidence advanced by special pleaders who set forth hypotheses in place of facts.

The anti-Shakespeareans base their arguments upon a few simple premises, all of them false. These false premises are that Shakespeare was an unlettered yokel without any schooling, that nothing is known about Shakespeare, and that only a noble lord or the equivalent in background could have written the plays. The facts are that more is known about Shakespeare than about most dramatists of his day, that he had a very good education, acquired in the Stratford Grammar School, that the plays show no evidence of profound book learning, and that the knowledge of kings and courts evident in the plays is no greater than any intelligent young man could have picked up at second hand. Most anti-Shakespeareans are naïve and betray an obvious snobbery. The author of their favorite plays, they imply, must have had a college diploma framed and hung on his study wall like the one in their dentist's office, and obviously so great a writer must have had a title or some equally significant evidence of exalted social background. They forget that genius has a way of cropping up in unexpected places and that none of the great creative writers of the world got his inspiration in a college or university course.

William Shakespeare was the son of John Shakespeare of Stratford-upon-Avon, a substantial citizen of that small but busy market town in the center of the rich agricultural county of Warwick. John Shakespeare kept a shop, what we would call a general store; he dealt in wool and other produce and gradually acquired property. As a youth, John Shakespeare had learned the trade of glover and leather worker. There is no contemporary evidence that the elder Shakespeare was a butcher, though the anti-Shakespeareans like to talk about the ignorant "butcher's boy of Stratford." Their only evidence is a statement by gossipy John Aubrey, more than a century after William Shakespeare's birth, that young William followed his father's trade, and when he killed a calf, "he would do it in a high style and make a speech." We would like to believe the story true, but Aubrey is not a very credible witness.

John Shakespeare probably continued to operate a farm at Snitterfield that his father had leased. He married Mary Arden, daughter of his father's landlord, a man of some property. The third of their eight children was William, baptized on April 26, 1564, and probably born three days before. At least, it is conventional to celebrate April 23 as his birthday.

The Stratford records give considerable information about John Shakespeare. We know that he held several municipal offices including those of alderman and mayor. In 1580 he was in some sort of legal difficulty and was fined for neglecting a summons of the Court of Queen's Bench requiring him to appear at Westminster and be bound over to keep the peace.

As a citizen and alderman of Stratford, John Shakespeare was entitled to send his son to the grammar school free. Though the records are lost, there can be no reason to doubt that this is where young William received his education. As any student of the period knows, the grammar schools provided the basic education in Latin learning and literature. The Elizabethan grammar school is not to be confused with modern grammar schools. Many

cultivated men of the day received all their formal
education in the grammar schools. At the universities in this period a student would have received
little training that would have inspired him to be a
creative writer. At Stratford young Shakespeare
would have acquired a familiarity with Latin and
some little knowledge of Greek. He would have
read Latin authors and become acquainted with
the plays of Plautus and Terence. Undoubtedly, in
this period of his life he received that stimulation
to read and explore for himself the world of ancient
and modern history which he later utilized in his
plays. The youngster who does not acquire this
type of intellectual curiosity *before* college days
rarely develops as a result of a college course the
kind of mind Shakespeare demonstrated. His learning in books was anything but profound, but he
clearly had the probing curiosity that sent him in
search of information, and he had a keenness in the
observation of nature and of humankind that finds
reflection in his poetry.

There is little documentation for Shakespeare's
boyhood. There is little reason why there should
be. Nobody knew that he was going to be a dramatist about whom any scrap of information would be
prized in the centuries to come. He was merely an
active and vigorous youth of Stratford, perhaps as-
sisting his father in his business, and no Boswell
bothered to write down facts about him. The most
important record that we have is a marriage license
issued by the Bishop of Worcester on November
27, 1582, to permit William Shakespeare to marry

Anne Hathaway, seven or eight years his senior; furthermore, the Bishop permitted the marriage after reading the banns only once instead of three times, evidence of the desire for haste. The need was explained on May 26, 1583, when the christening of Susanna, daughter of William and Anne Shakespeare, was recorded at Stratford. Two years later, on February 2, 1585, the records show the birth of twins to the Shakespeares, a boy and a girl who were christened Hamnet and Judith.

What William Shakespeare was doing in Stratford during the early years of his married life, or when he went to London, we do not know. It has been conjectured that he tried his hand at schoolteaching, but that is a mere guess. There is a legend that he left Stratford to escape a charge of poaching in the park of Sir Thomas Lucy of Charlecote, but there is no proof of this. There is also a legend that when first he came to London he earned his living by holding horses outside a playhouse and presently was given employment inside, but there is nothing better than eighteenth-century hearsay for this. How Shakespeare broke into the London theatres as a dramatist and actor we do not know. But lack of information is not surprising, for Elizabethans did not write their autobiographies, and we know even less about the lives of many writers and some men of affairs than we know about Shakespeare. By 1592 he was so well established and popular that he incurred the envy of the dramatist and pamphleteer Robert Greene, who referred to him as an "upstart crow . . . in his own

conceit the only Shake-scene in a country." From
this time onward, contemporary allusions and references in legal documents enable the scholar to
chart Shakespeare's career with greater accuracy
than is possible with most other Elizabethan dramatists.

By 1594 Shakespeare was a member of the company of actors known as the Lord Chamberlain's
Men. After the accession of James I, in 1603, the
company would have the sovereign for their patron
and would be known as the King's Men. During the
period of its greatest prosperity, this company
would have as its principal theatres the Globe and
the Blackfriars. Shakespeare was both an actor and
a shareholder in the company. Tradition has as-
signed him such acting roles as Adam in *As You
Like It* and the Ghost in *Hamlet,* a modest place
on the stage that suggests that he may have had
other duties in the management of the company.
Such conclusions, however, are based on surmise.

What we do know is that his plays were popular
and that he was highly successful in his vocation.
His first play may have been *The Comedy of Errors,* acted perhaps in 1591. Certainly this was one
of his earliest plays. The three parts of *Henry VI*
were acted sometime between 1590 and 1592.
Critics are not in agreement about precisely how
much Shakespeare wrote of these three plays.
Richard III probably dates from 1593. With this
play Shakespeare captured the imagination of Elizabethan audiences, then enormously interested in
historical plays. With *Richard III* Shakespeare also

gave an interpretation pleasing to the Tudors of the rise to power of the grandfather of Queen Elizabeth. From this time onward, Shakespeare's plays followed on the stage in rapid succession: *Titus Andronicus, The Taming of the Shrew, The Two Gentlemen of Verona, Love's Labor's Lost, Romeo and Juliet, Richard II, A Midsummer Night's Dream, King John, The Merchant of Venice, Henry IV (Parts 1 and 2), Much Ado about Nothing, Henry V, Julius Cæsar, As You Like It, Twelfth Night, Hamlet, The Merry Wives of Windsor, All's Well That Ends Well, Measure for Measure, Othello, King Lear,* and nine others that followed before Shakespeare retired completely, about 1613.

In the course of his career in London, he made enough money to enable him to retire to Stratford with a competence. His purchase on May 4, 1597, of New Place, then the second-largest dwelling in Stratford, "a pretty house of brick and timber," with a handsome garden, indicates his increasing prosperity. There his wife and children lived while he busied himself in the London theatres. The summer before he acquired New Place, his life was darkened by the death of his only son, Hamnet, a child of eleven. In May, 1602, Shakespeare purchased one hundred and seven acres of fertile farmland near Stratford and a few months later bought a cottage and garden across the alley from New Place. About 1611, he seems to have returned permanently to Stratford, for the next year a legal document refers to him as "William Shakespeare of Stratford-upon-Avon . . . gentleman." To achieve

⌈28⌋

*Shakespear ye Player
by Garter*

clement apoldut by Garter

**A sketch of the coat of arms granted to William Shakespeare by
William Dethick, Garter King of Arms, in 1596.
Folger MS (V.a. 156.)**

the desired appellation of gentleman, William Shakespeare had seen to it that the College of Heralds in 1596 granted his father a coat of arms. In one step he thus became a second-generation gentleman.

Shakespeare's daughter Susanna made a good match in 1607 with Dr. John Hall, a prominent and prosperous Stratford physician. His second daughter, Judith, did not marry until she was thirty-one years old, and then, under somewhat scandalous circumstances, she married Thomas Quiney, a Stratford vintner. On March 25, 1616, Shakespeare made his will, bequeathing his landed property to Susanna, £300 to Judith, certain sums to other relatives, and his second-best bed to his wife, Anne. Much has been made of the second-best bed, but the legacy probably indicates only that Anne liked that particular bed. Shakespeare, following the practice of the time, may have already arranged with Susanna for his wife's care. Finally, on April 23, 1616, the anniversary of his birth, William Shakespeare died, and he was buried on April 25 within the chancel of Trinity Church, as befitted an honored citizen. On August 6, 1623, a few months before the publication of the collected edition of Shakespeare's plays, Anne Shakespeare joined her husband in death.

During his lifetime Shakespeare made no effort to publish any of his plays, though eighteen appeared in print in single-play editions known as quartos. Some of these are corrupt versions known as "bad quartos." No quarto, so far as is known, had the author's approval. Plays were not considered "literature" any more than most radio and television scripts today are considered literature. Dramatists sold their plays outright to the theatrical companies and it was usually considered in the company's interest to keep plays from getting into print. To achieve a reputation as a man of letters, Shakespeare wrote his *Sonnets* and his narrative poems, *Venus and Adonis* and *The Rape of Lucrece,* but he probably never dreamed that his plays would establish his reputation as a literary genius. Only Ben Jonson, a man known for his colossal conceit, had the crust to call his plays *Works,* as he did when he published an edition in 1616. But men laughed at Ben Jonson.

After Shakespeare's death, two of his old colleagues in the King's Men, John Heminges and Henry Condell, decided that it would be a good thing to print, in more accurate versions than were then available, the plays already published and eighteen additional plays not previously published in quarto. In 1623 appeared *Mr. William Shakespeares Comedies, Histories, & Tragedies. Pub-*

*lished according to the True Originall Copies.
London. Printed by Isaac Iaggard and Ed. Blount.*
This was the famous First Folio, a work that had the
authority of Shakespeare's associates. The only play
commonly attributed to Shakespeare that was omit-
ted in the First Folio was *Pericles*. In their preface,
"To the great Variety of Readers," Heminges and
Condell state that whereas "you were abused with
diverse stolen and surreptitious copies, maimed and
deformed by the frauds and stealths of injurious
impostors that exposed them, even those are now
offered to your view cured and perfect of their
limbs; and all the rest, absolute in their numbers,
as he conceived them." What they used for printer's copy is one of the vexed problems of scholarship, and skilled bibliographers have devoted years
of study to the question of the relation of the "copy"
for the First Folio to Shakespeare's manuscripts. In
some cases it is clear that the editors corrected
printed quarto versions of the plays, probably by
comparison with playhouse scripts. Whether these
scripts were in Shakespeare's autograph is any-
body's guess. No manuscript of any play in Shakespeare's handwriting has survived. Indeed, very few
play manuscripts from this period by any author are
extant. The Tudor and Stuart periods had not yet
learned to prize autographs and authors' original
manuscripts.

Since the First Folio contains eighteen plays not
previously printed, it is the only source for these.
For the other eighteen, which had appeared in
quarto versions, the First Folio also has the author-

ity of an edition prepared and overseen by Shakespeare's colleagues and professional associates. But since editorial standards in 1623 were far from strict, and Heminges and Condell were actors rather than editors by profession, the texts are sometimes careless. The printing and proofreading of the First Folio also left much to be desired, and some garbled passages have had to be corrected and emended. The "good quarto" texts have to be taken into account in preparing a modern edition.

Because of the great popularity of Shakespeare through the centuries, the First Folio has become a prized book, but it is not a very rare one, for it is estimated that 238 copies are extant. The Folger Shakespeare Library in Washington, D.C., has seventy-nine copies of the First Folio, collected by the founder, Henry Clay Folger, who believed that a collation of as many texts as possible would reveal significant facts about the text of Shakespeare's plays. Dr. Charlton Hinman, using an ingenious machine of his own invention for mechanical collating, has made many discoveries that throw light on Shakespeare's text and on printing practices of the day.

The probability is that the First Folio of 1623 had an edition of between 1,000 and 1,250 copies. It is believed that it sold for £1, which made it an expensive book, for £1 in 1623 was equivalent to something between $40 and $50 in modern purchasing power.

During the seventeenth century, Shakespeare was sufficiently popular to warrant three later editions in folio size, the Second Folio of 1632, the Third Folio of 1663–1664, and the Fourth Folio of 1685. The Third Folio added six other plays ascribed to Shakespeare, but these are apocryphal.

THE SHAKESPEAREAN THEATRE

The theatres in which Shakespeare's plays were performed were vastly different from those we know today. The stage was a platform that jutted out into the area now occupied by the first rows of seats on the main floor, what is called the "orchestra" in America and the "pit" in England. This platform had no curtain to come down at the ends of acts and scenes. And although simple stage properties were available, the Elizabethan theatre lacked both the machinery and the elaborate movable scenery of the modern theatre. In the rear of the platform stage was a curtained area that could be used as an inner room, a tomb, or any such scene that might be required. A balcony above this inner room, and perhaps balconies on the sides of the stage, could represent the upper deck of a ship, the entry to Juliet's room, or a prison window. A trap door in the stage provided an entrance for ghosts and devils from the nether regions, and a similar trap in the canopied structure over the stage, known as the "heavens," made it possible to let down angels on a rope. These primitive stage arrangements help to account for many elements in Elizabethan plays. For example, since there was no curtain, the dramatist frequently felt the necessity of writing into his play action to clear the stage at the ends of acts and scenes. The funeral march at the end of *Hamlet* is not there merely for atmosphere; Shakespeare had to get the corpses off the stage. The lack of scenery also freed the dramatist from undue concern about the exact location of his sets, and the physical relation of his various settings to each other did not have to be worked out with the same precision as in the modern theatre.

Before London had buildings designed exclusively for theatrical entertainment, plays were given in inns and taverns. The characteristic inn of the period had an inner courtyard with rooms opening onto balconies overlooking the yard. Players could set up their temporary stages at one end of the yard and audiences could find seats on the balconies out of the weather. The poorer sort could stand or sit on the cobblestones in the yard, which was open to the sky. The first theatres followed this construction, and throughout the Elizabethan period the large public theatres had a yard in front of the stage open to the weather, with two or three tiers of covered balconies extending around the theatre. This physical structure again influenced the writing of plays. Because a dramatist wanted the actors to be heard, he frequently wrote into his play orations that could be delivered with declamatory effect. He also provided spectacle, buffoonery, and broad jests to keep the riotous groundlings in the yard entertained and quiet.

In another respect the Elizabethan theatre differed greatly from ours. It had no actresses. All women's roles were taken by boys, sometimes recruited from the boys' choirs of the London churches. Some of these youths acted their roles with great skill and the Elizabethans did not seem to be aware of any incongruity. The first actresses on the professional English stage appeared after the Restoration of Charles II, in 1660, when exiled Englishmen brought back from France practices of the French stage.

London in the Elizabethan period, as now, was the center of theatrical interest, though wandering actors from time to time traveled through the country performing in inns, halls, and the houses of the nobility. The first professional playhouse, called simply The Theatre, was erected by James Burbage, father of Shakespeare's colleague Richard Burbage, in 1576 on lands of the old Holywell Priory adjacent to Finsbury Fields, a playground and park area just north of the city walls. It had the advantage of being outside the city's jurisdiction and yet was near enough to be easily accessible. Soon after The Theatre was opened, another playhouse called The Curtain was erected in the same neighborhood. Both of these playhouses had open courtyards and were probably polygonal in shape.

About the time The Curtain opened, Richard Farrant, Master of the Children of the Chapel Royal at Windsor and of St. Paul's, conceived the idea of opening a "private" theatre in the old monastery buildings of the Blackfriars, not far from St. Paul's Cathedral in the heart of the city. This theatre was ostensibly to train the choirboys in plays for presentation at Court, but Farrant managed to present plays to paying audiences and achieved considerable success until aristocratic neighbors complained and had the theatre closed. This first Blackfriars Theatre was significant, however, because it popularized the boy actors in a professional way and it paved the way for a second theatre in the Blackfriars, which Shakespeare's company took over more than thirty years later. By the last years of the sixteenth century, London had at least six professional theatres and still others were erected during the reign of James I.

The Globe Theatre, the playhouse that most people connect with Shakespeare, was erected early in 1599 on the Bankside, the area across the Thames from the city. Its construction had a dramatic beginning, for on the night of December 28, 1598, James Burbage's sons, Cuthbert and Richard, gathered together a crew who tore down the old theatre in Holywell and carted the timbers across the river to a site that they had chosen for a new playhouse. The reason for this clandestine operation was a row with the landowner over the lease to the Holywell property. The site chosen for the Globe was another playground outside of the city's jurisdiction, a region of somewhat unsavory character. Not far away was the Bear Garden, an amphitheatre devoted to the baiting of bears and bulls. This was also the region occupied by many houses of ill fame licensed by the Bishop of Winchester and the source of substantial revenue to him. But it was easily accessible either from London Bridge or by means of the cheap boats operated by the London watermen, and it had the great advantage of being beyond the authority of the Puritanical aldermen of London, who frowned on plays because they lured apprentices from work, filled their heads with improper ideas, and generally exerted a bad influence. The aldermen also complained that the crowds drawn together in the theatre helped to spread the plague.

The Globe was the handsomest theatre up to its time. It was a large building, apparently octagonal in shape, and open like its predecessors to the sky in the center, but capable of seating a large audience in its covered balconies. To erect and operate the Globe, the Burbages organized a syndicate composed of the leading members of the dramatic company, of which Shakespeare was a member. Since it was open to the weather and depended on natural light, plays had to be given in the afternoon. This caused no hardship in the long afternoons of an English summer, but in the winter the weather was a great handicap and discouraged all except the hardiest. For that reason, in 1608 Shakespeare's company was glad to take over the lease of the second Blackfriars Theatre, a substantial, roomy hall reconstructed within the framework of the old monastery building. This theatre was protected from the weather and its stage was artificially lighted by chandeliers of candles. This became the winter playhouse for Shakespeare's company and at once proved so popular that the congestion of traffic

created an embarrassing problem. Stringent regula-
tions had to be made for the movement of coaches
in the vicinity. Shakespeare's company continued to
use the Globe during the summer months. In 1613
a squib fired from a cannon during a performance
of *Henry VIII* fell on the thatched roof and the
Globe burned to the ground. The next year it was
rebuilt.

London had other famous theatres. The Rose, just
west of the Globe, was built by Philip Henslowe, a
semiliterate denizen of the Bankside, who became
one of the most important theatrical owners and
producers of the Tudor and Stuart periods. What is
more important for historians, he kept a detailed account book, which provides much of our information
about theatrical history in his time. Another famous
theatre on the Bankside was the Swan, which a
Dutch priest, Johannes de Witt, visited in 1596. The
crude drawing of the stage which he made was
copied by his friend Arend van Buchell; it is one of
the important pieces of contemporary evidence for
cheatrical construction. Among the other theatres,
the Fortune, north of the city, on Golding Lane,
and the Red Bull, even farther away from the city,
off St. John's Street, were the most popular. The
Red Bull, much frequented by apprentices, favored
sensational and sometimes rowdy plays.

The actors who kept all of these theatres going
were organized into companies under the protection
of some noble patron. Traditionally actors had enjoyed a low reputation. In some of the ordinances
they were classed as vagrants; in the phraseology

of the time, "rogues, vagabonds, sturdy beggars, and common players" were all listed together as undesirables. To escape penalties often meted out to these characters, organized groups of actors managed to gain the protection of various personages of high degree. In the later years of Elizabeth's reign, a group flourished under the name of the Queen's Men; another group had the protection of the Lord Admiral and were known as the Lord Admiral's Men. Edward Alleyn, son-in-law of Philip Henslowe, was the leading spirit in the Lord Admiral's Men. Besides the adult companies, troupes of boy actors from time to time also enjoyed considerable popularity. Among these were the Children of Paul's and the Children of the Chapel Royal.

The company with which Shakespeare had a long association had for its first patron Henry Carey, Lord Hunsdon, the Lord Chamberlain, and hence they were known as the Lord Chamberlain's Men. After the accession of James I, they became the King's Men. This company was the great rival of the Lord Admiral's Men, managed by Henslowe and Alleyn.

All was not easy for the players in Shakespeare's time, for the aldermen of London were always eager for an excuse to close up the Blackfriars and any other theatres in their jurisdiction. The theatres outside the jurisdiction of London were not immune from interference, for they might be shut up by order of the Privy Council for meddling in politics or for various other offenses, or they might be closed in time of plague lest they spread infection.

During plague times, the actors usually went on tour and played the provinces wherever they could find an audience. Particularly frightening were the plagues of 1592–1594 and 1613 when the theatres closed and the players, like many other Londoners, had to take to the country.

Though players had a low social status, they enjoyed great popularity, and one of the favorite forms of entertainment at Court was the performance of plays. To be commanded to perform at Court conferred great prestige upon a company of players, and printers frequently noted that fact when they published plays. Several of Shakespeare's plays were performed before the sovereign, and Shakespeare himself undoubtedly acted in some of these plays.

REFERENCES FOR FURTHER READING

Many readers will want suggestions for further reading about Shakespeare and his times. A few references will serve as guides to further study in the enormous literature on the subject. A simple and useful little book is Gerald Sanders, *A Shakespeare Primer* (New York, 1950). *A Companion to Shakespeare Studies,* edited by Harley Granville-Barker and G. B. Harrison (Cambridge, 1934), is a valuable guide. The most recent concise handbook of facts about Shakespeare is Gerald E. Bentley, *Shakespeare: A Biographical Handbook* (New Haven, 1961). More detailed but not so voluminous as to be confusing is Hazelton Spencer, *The Art and Life of William Shakespeare* (New York, 1940), which, like Sanders' and Bentley's handbooks, contains a brief annotated list of useful books on various aspects of the subject. The most detailed and scholarly work providing complete factual information about Shakespeare is Sir Edmund Chambers, *William Shakespeare: A Study of Facts and Problems* (2 vols., Oxford, 1930).

Among other biographies of Shakespeare, Joseph Quincy Adams, *A Life of William Shakespeare* (Boston, 1923) is still an excellent assessment of the essential facts and the traditional information, and Marchette Chute, *Shakespeare of London* (New York, 1949; paperback, 1957) stresses Shakespeare's life in the theatre. Two new biographies of Shakespeare have recently appeared. A. L. Rowse, *William Shakespeare: A Biography* (London, 1963; New York, 1964) provides an appraisal by a distinguished English historian, who dismisses the notion that somebody else wrote Shakespeare's plays as arrant nonsense that runs counter to known historical fact. Peter Quennell, *Shakespeare: A Biography* (Cleveland and New York, 1963) is a sensitive and intelligent survey of what is known and surmised of Shakespeare's life. Louis B. Wright, *Shakespeare for Everyman* (New York, 1964; 1965) discusses the basis of Shakespeare's enduring popularity.

The Shakespeare Quarterly, published by the Shakespeare Association of America under the editorship of James G. McManaway, is recommended for those who wish to keep up with current Shakespearean scholarship and stage productions. The *Quarterly* includes an annual bibliography of Shakespeare editions and works on Shakespeare published during the previous year.

The question of the authenticity of Shakespeare's plays arouses perennial attention. The theory of hidden cryptograms in the plays is demolished by William F. and Elizebeth S. Friedman, *The Shakespearean Ciphers Examined* (New York, 1957). A succinct account of the various absurdities advanced to suggest the authorship of a multitude of candidates other than Shakespeare will be found in R. C. Churchill, *Shakespeare and His Betters* (Bloomington, Ind., 1959). Another recent discussion of the subject, *The Authorship of Shakespeare*, by James G. McManaway (Washington, D.C., 1962), presents the evidence from contemporary records to prove the identity of Shakespeare the actor-playwright with Shakespeare of Stratford.

Scholars are not in agreement about the details of playhouse construction in the Elizabethan period. John C. Adams presents a plausible reconstruction of the Globe in *The Globe Playhouse: Its Design and Equipment* (Cambridge, Mass., 1942; 2nd rev. ed., 1961). A description with excellent drawings based on Dr. Adams' model is Irwin Smith, *Shakespeare's Globe Playhouse: A Modern Reconstruction in Text and Scale Drawings* (New York, 1956). Other sensible discussions are C. Walter Hodges, *The Globe Restored* (London, 1953) and A. M. Nagler, *Shakespeare's Stage* (New Haven, 1958). Bernard Beckerman, *Shakespeare at the Globe*,

1599–1609 (New Haven, 1962; paperback, 1962) discusses Elizabethan staging and acting techniques.

A sound and readable history of the early theatres is Joseph Quincy Adams, *Shakespearean Playhouses: A History of English Theatres from the Beginnings to the Restoration* (Boston, 1917). For detailed, factual information about the Elizabethan and seventeenth-century stages, the definitive reference works are Sir Edmund Chambers, *The Elizabethan Stage* (4 vols., Oxford, 1923) and Gerald E. Bentley, *The Jacobean and Caroline Stages* (5 vols., Oxford, 1941–1956).

Further information on the history of the theatre and related topics will be found in the following titles: T. W. Baldwin, *The Organization and Personnel of the Shakespearean Company* (Princeton, 1927); Lily Bess Campbell, *Scenes and Machines on the English Stage during the Renaissance* (Cambridge, 1923); Esther Cloudman Dunn, *Shakespeare in America* (New York, 1939); George C. D. Odell, *Shakespeare from Betterton to Irving* (2 vols., London, 1931); Arthur Colby Sprague, *Shakespeare and the Actors: The Stage Business in His Plays (1660–1905)* (Cambridge, Mass., 1944) and *Shakespearian Players and Performances* (Cambridge, Mass., 1953); Leslie Hotson, *The Commonwealth and Restoration Stage* (Cambridge, Mass., 1928); Alwin Thaler, *Shakspere to Sheridan: A Book about the Theatre of Yesterday and To-day* (Cambridge, Mass., 1922); George C. Branam, *Eighteenth-Century Adaptations of Shakespeare's Tragedies* (Berkeley, 1956); C. Beecher Hogan, *Shakespeare in the*

Theatre, 1701–1800 (Oxford, 1957); Ernest Bradlee
Watson, *Sheridan to Robertson: A Study of the 19th-
Century London Stage* (Cambridge, Mass., 1926);
and Enid Welsford, *The Court Masque* (Cambridge, Mass., 1927).

A brief account of the growth of Shakespeare's
reputation is F. E. Halliday, *The Cult of Shakespeare* (London, 1947). A more detailed discussion
is given in Augustus Ralli, *A History of Shakespearian Criticism* (2 vols., Oxford, 1932; New York,
1958). Harley Granville-Barker, *Prefaces to Shakespeare* (5 vols., London, 1927–1948; 2 vols., London,
1958) provides stimulating critical discussion of the
plays. An older classic of criticism is Andrew C.
Bradley, *Shakespearean Tragedy: Lectures on Hamlet, Othello, King Lear, Macbeth* (London, 1904;
paperback, 1955). Sir Edmund Chambers, *Shakespeare: A Survey* (London, 1935; paperback, 1958)
contains short, sensible essays on thirty-four of the
plays, originally written as introductions to single-
play editions. Alfred Harbage, *William Shakespeare:
A Reader's Guide* (New York, 1963) is a handbook
to the reading and appreciation of the plays, with
scene synopses and interpretation.

For the history plays see Lily Bess Campbell,
*Shakespeare's "Histories": Mirrors of Elizabethan
Policy* (Cambridge, 1947); John Palmer, *Political
Characters of Shakespeare* (London, 1945; 1961);
E. M. W. Tillyard, *Shakespeare's History Plays*
(London, 1948); Irving Ribner, *The English History
Play in the Age of Shakespeare* (Princeton, 1947);
Max M. Reese, *The Cease of Majesty* (London,

1961); and Arthur Colby Sprague, *Shakespeare's Histories: Plays for the Stage* (London, 1964). Harold Jenkins, "Shakespeare's History Plays: 1900–1951," *Shakespeare Survey 6* (Cambridge, 1953), 1–15, provides an excellent survey of recent critical opinion on the subject.

In addition to the titles listed above, a number of other works provide critical and historical background for study of the *Henry VI* plays. Paul M. Kendall, *The Yorkist Age: Daily Life during the Wars of the Roses* (New York, 1962) devotes a chapter to a lucid summary of the course of the conflict between York and Lancaster and describes the various battles. S. B. Chrimes, *Lancastrians, Yorkists, and Henry VII* (London & New York, 1964) presents a full explication of the dynastic problem resulting from Edward III's many children and the course of events leading up to Henry VII's assumption of the throne. C. L. Kingsford, *Prejudice and Promise in Fifteenth Century England* (Oxford, 1925) has a valuable chapter on Shakespeare's treatment of fifteenth-century English history. Hereward T. Price, *Construction in Shakespeare*, University of Michigan Contributions in Modern Philology, No. 17 (Ann Arbor, 1951), argues for a unified pattern to the three parts of *Henry VI* and Shakespeare's sole authorship and defends the skill of their construction. The most recent edition of the trilogy has been edited by Andrew S. Cairncross for the new Arden series (3 vols., London & Cambridge, Mass., 1962–1964).

The comedies are illuminated by the following

studies: C. L. Barber, *Shakespeare's Festive Comedy* (Princeton, 1959); John Russell Brown, *Shakespeare and His Comedies* (London, 1957); H. B. Charlton, *Shakespearian Comedy* (London, 1938; 4th ed., 1949); W. W. Lawrence, *Shakespeare's Problem Comedies* (New York, 1931); and Thomas M. Parrott, *Shakespearean Comedy* (New York, 1949).

Further discussions of Shakespeare's tragedies, in addition to Bradley, already cited, are contained in H. B. Charlton, *Shakespearian Tragedy* (Cambridge, 1948); Willard Farnham, *The Medieval Heritage of Elizabethan Tragedy* (Berkeley, 1936) and *Shakespeare's Tragic Frontier: The World of His Final Tragedies* (Berkeley, 1950); and Harold S. Wilson, *On the Design of Shakespearian Tragedy* (Toronto, 1957).

The "Roman" plays are treated in M. M. MacCallum, *Shakespeare's Roman Plays and Their Background* (London, 1910) and J. C. Maxwell, "Shakespeare's Roman Plays, 1900–1956," *Shakespeare Survey 10* (Cambridge, 1957), 1–11.

Kenneth Muir, *Shakespeare's Sources: Comedies and Tragedies* (London, 1957) discusses Shakespeare's use of source material. The sources themselves have been reprinted several times. Among old editions are John P. Collier (ed.), *Shakespeare's Library* (2 vols., London, 1850), Israel C. Gollancz (ed.), *The Shakespeare Classics* (12 vols., London, 1907–1926), and W. C. Hazlitt (ed.), *Shakespeare's Library* (6 vols., London, 1875). A modern edition is being prepared by Geoffrey Bullough with the title *Narrative and Dramatic Sources of Shakespeare*

(London and New York, 1957–). Five volumes, covering the sources for the comedies, histories, and Roman plays, have been published to date (1966).

In addition to the second edition of *Webster's New International Dictionary*, which contains most of the unusual words used by Shakespeare, the following reference works are helpful: Edwin A. Abbott, *A Shakespearian Grammar* (London, 1872); C. T. Onions, *A Shakespeare Glossary* (2nd rev. ed., Oxford, 1925); and Eric Partridge, *Shakespeare's Bawdy* (New York, 1948; paperback, 1960).

Some knowledge of the social background of the period in which Shakespeare lived is important for a full understanding of his work. A brief, clear, and accurate account of Tudor history is S. T. Bindoff, *The Tudors,* in the Penguin series. A readable general history is G. M. Trevelyan, *The History of England,* first published in 1926 and available in numerous editions. The same author's *English Social History,* first published in 1942 and also available in many editions, provides fascinating information about England in all periods. Sir John Neale, *Queen Elizabeth* (London, 1935; paperback, 1957) is the best study of the great Queen. Various aspects of life in the Elizabethan period are treated in Louis B. Wright, *Middle-Class Culture in Elizabethan England* (Chapel Hill, N.C., 1935; reprinted Ithaca, N.Y., 1958, 1964). *Shakespeare's England: An Account of the Life and Manners of His Age,* edited by Sidney Lee and C. T. Onions (2 vols., Oxford, 1917), provides much information on many aspects of Elizabethan life. A fascinating survey of the period will be found in Muriel St. C. Byrne, *Elizabethan Life in Town and Country* (London, 1925; rev. ed., 1954; paperback, 1961).

The Folger Library is issuing a series of illustrated booklets entitled "Folger Booklets on Tudor and Stuart Civilization," printed and distributed by Cornell University Press. Published to date are the following titles:

D. W. Davies, *Dutch Influences on English Culture, 1558–1625*

Giles E. Dawson, *The Life of William Shakespeare*

Ellen C. Eyler, *Early English Gardens and Garden Books*

Elaine W. Fowler, *English Sea Power in the Early Tudor Period, 1485–1558*

John R. Hale, *The Art of War and Renaissance England*

William Haller, *Elizabeth I and the Puritans*

Virginia A. LaMar, *English Dress in the Age of Shakespeare*

———, *Travel and Roads in England*

John L. Lievsay, *The Elizabethan Image of Italy*

James G. McManaway, *The Authorship of Shakespeare*

Dorothy E. Mason, *Music in Elizabethan England*

Garrett Mattingly, *The "Invincible" Armada and Elizabethan England*

Boies Penrose, *Tudor and Early Stuart Voyaging*

T. I. Rae, *Scotland in the Time of Shakespeare*

Conyers Read, *The Government of England under Elizabeth*

Albert J. Schmidt, *The Yeoman in Tudor and Stuart England*

Lilly C. Stone, *English Sports and Recreations*

Craig R. Thompson, *The Bible in English, 1525–1611*

———, *The English Church in the Sixteenth Century*

———, *Schools in Tudor England*

———, *Universities in Tudor England*

Louis B. Wright, *Shakespeare's Theatre and the Dramatic Tradition*

At intervals the Folger Library plans to gather these booklets in hardbound volumes. The first is *Life and Letters in Tudor and Stuart England, First Folger Series*, edited by Louis B. Wright and Virginia A. LaMar (published for the Folger Shakespeare Library by Cornell University Press, 1962). The volume contains eleven of the separate booklets.

Actual Chronology for Events in the Three Parts of Henry VI

1421
Dec. 6   Birth of Henry VI at Windsor.

1422
Aug. 31   Death of Henry V at Vincennes.

Oct. 21   Charles VI of France dies, succeeded by Charles VII.

Nov. 7   Body of Henry V lies in state in Westminster Abbey.

Nov. 9   Parliament summoned.

1423
Aug. 1   Salisbury defeats French at Cravant.

1424
Aug. 17   Bedford defeats French at Verneuil.

1425
Aug. 2   Salisbury takes Le Mans.

Oct. 1   Gloucester and Winchester clash in London.

1427
Sept. 5   Dunois, Bastard of Orléans, defeats English at Montargis.

1429
May 1–3   Joan of Arc raises the siege of Orléans.

July 17   Charles VII crowned at Reims.

Nov. 6   Henry VI crowned at Westminster.

1430
May 23   Joan of Arc captured at Compiègne.

1431
May 30   Joan of Arc burned at Rouen.

Dec. 16	Henry VI crowned in Notre Dame, Paris.
1435	
Sept. 15	Death of John, Duke of Bedford.
1436	French recover Paris.
1444	
May 28	Two-year Anglo-French truce signed at Tours.
1445	
April 22	Henry VI marries Margaret of Anjou.
1448	
May	French recover Maine and Anjou by marriage treaty.
1450–54	Jack Cade's Rebellion.
1451	French conquer Guienne.
1453	English retain only Calais and Channel Islands of French possessions.
1454	
March 27	Richard, Duke of York, made Protector.
1455	
May 22	1st Battle of St. Albans; Yorkist victory.
1460	
July 10	Battle of Northampton; Yorkist victory.
Dec. 30	Battle of Wakefield; Lancastrian victory; death of Duke of York.
1461	
Feb. 2	Battle of Mortimer's Cross; Yorkist victory.
Feb. 17	2nd Battle of St. Albans; Lancastrian victory.
March 1	Edward, Earl of March, acclaimed King in London.

March 29   Battle of Towton; rout of Lancastrians.

June 28   Coronation of Edward IV; Henry VI and Margaret of Anjou retire to Scotland.

July 22   Death of Charles VII of France; succeeded by Louis XI.

1469
July 26   Battle of Banbury; victory of Warwick against forces of Edward IV.

1470
Oct. 13   Henry VI restored to throne.

1471
April 14   Battle of Barnet; Yorkist victory; death of Earl of Warwick.

May 4   Battle of Tewkesbury; decisive Yorkist victory; death of Edward, Prince of Wales.

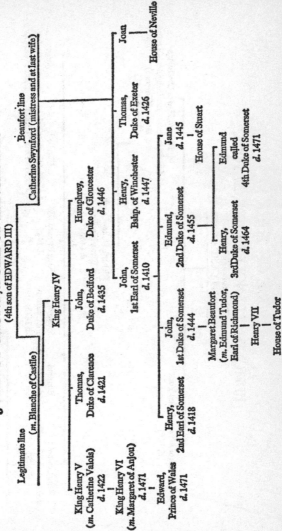

HOUSE OF LANCASTER

JOHN OF GAUNT, DUKE OF LANCASTER
(4th son of EDWARD III)

Legitimate line (m. Blanche of Castile)

Beaufort line (Catherine Swynford (mistress and at last wife))

King Henry IV

King Henry V (m. Catherine Valois) d.1422
— King Henry VI (m. Margaret of Anjou) d.1471
— Edward, Prince of Wales d.1471

Thomas, Duke of Clarence d.1421

John, Duke of Bedford d.1435

Humphrey, Duke of Gloucester d.1446

John, 1st Earl of Somerset d.1410

Henry, Bishp. of Winchester d.1447

Thomas, Duke of Exeter d.1426

Joan — House of Neville

Henry, 2nd Earl of Somerset d.1418

John, 1st Duke of Somerset d.1444
— Margaret Beaufort (m. Edmund Tudor, Earl of Richmond)
— Henry VII
— House of Tudor

Edmund, 2nd Duke of Somerset d.1455
— Henry, 3rd Duke of Somerset d.1464

Jane d.1445 — House of Stuart

Edmund called 4th Duke of Somerset d.1471

HOUSE OF YORK

EDMUND OF LANGLEY, DUKE OF YORK

(5th son of EDWARD III)
(m. ISABELLA of CASTILE)

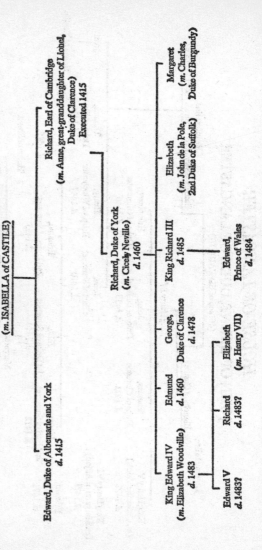

HOUSE OF MORTIMER

LIONEL, DUKE OF CLARENCE

(3rd son of EDWARD III)
(m. ELIZABETH de BURGH)

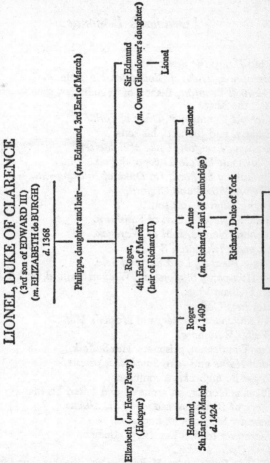

[Dramatis Personae

King Henry the Sixth.

Humphrey, Duke of Gloucester, his uncle.

Cardinal Beaufort, Bishop of Winchester, great-uncle to the *King.*

Richard Plantagenet, Duke of York.

Edward and *Richard,* his sons.

Edmund Beaufort, Duke of Somerset.

William de la Pole, Duke of Suffolk.

Humphrey Stafford, 1st Duke of Buckingham.

Thomas, 8th Baron Clifford.

Young Clifford, his son.

Richard Neville, Earl of Salisbury.

Richard Neville, Earl of Warwick.

Thomas, 7th Baron Scales.

James Fiennes, Lord Say and Sele.

Sir Humphrey Stafford and *William Stafford,* his brother.

Sir William Vaux.

Matthew Goffe.

A Lieutenant, Master, and *Master's Mate.*

Walter Whitmore.

Two Gentlemen, prisoners with *Suffolk.*

John Hume and *John Southwell,* priests.

Roger Bolingbroke, a conjurer.

Thomas Horner, an armorer, and *Peter,* his man.

Clerk of Chatham. Mayor of St. Albans.

Saunder Simpcox, an impostor.

Alexander Iden, a Kentish gentleman.

Jack Cade, a rebel.

George Bevis, John Holland, Dick the butcher, *Smith* the weaver, *Michael,* and other followers of *Cade.*

Two Murderers.

Margaret, Queen to *King Henry.*
Eleanor, Duchess of Gloucester.
Margery Jourdain, a witch.
Wife to Simpcox.
Lords, Ladies, and Attendants, Petitioners, Aldermen, a
Herald, a Beadle, Sheriff and Officers, Gentlemen, Citi-
zens, 'Prentices, Falconers, Guards, Soldiers, Messengers,
etc.
A Spirit.

SCENE: England]

THE SECOND PART
OF
HENRY THE SIXTH

ACT I

I.i. Suffolk delivers Margaret of Anjou to the delighted King. The nobility, however, are displeased when they learn that the articles of peace include the return of Anjou and Maine and that she brings no dowry. Gloucester voices his distress to the other members of the King's Council. Although they agree with him on this point, behind his back Cardinal Beaufort urges the rest to join with him in bringing about Gloucester's downfall. The others have no more liking for the Cardinal than they have for Gloucester. Only Salisbury and his son, the Earl of Warwick, express more concern for the country's welfare than for their private ambitions. York is particularly disgruntled at the loss of Anjou and Maine, since he considers himself the rightful sovereign and feels that Suffolk and the King have given away his territories. He vows to bide his time until he sees a favorable opportunity to seize the crown.

▬▬▬▬▬▬▬▬▬▬▬▬▬▬

Ent. **hautboys:** oboes.

1. **imperial:** an adjective appropriate to one who claimed dominion over England, France, and Ireland.

2. **had in charge:** was charged to do; **depart:** departure.

3. **procurator:** agent; proxy.

5. **Tours:** a conference was held at Tours in 1444, which resulted in a truce between England and France and the betrothal of Margaret and King Henry, with Suffolk acting as proxy. The proxy marriage took place in the following year at Nancy.

7. **Calaber:** Calabria.

14. **title:** legal claim.

ACT I

Scene I. [London. The palace.]

Flourish of trumpets, then hautboys. Enter King, Duke Humphrey, Salisbury, Warwick, and [Cardinal] Beaufort, on the one side; the Queen, Suffolk, York, Somerset, and Buckingham, on the other.

Suf. As by your high imperial Majesty
I had in charge at my depart for France,
As procurator to your Excellence,
To marry Princess Margaret for your Grace,
So, in the famous ancient city Tours, 5
In presence of the Kings of France and Sicil,
The Dukes of Orléans, Calaber, Bretagne, and
    Alençon,
Seven earls, twelve barons, and twenty reverend
    bishops, 10
I have performed my task and was espoused:
And humbly now upon my bended knee,
In sight of England and her lordly peers,
Deliver up my title in the Queen
To your most gracious hands, that are the substance 15
Of that great shadow I did represent;

20. **kinder:** more natural.

28. **mutual:** intimate; **conference:** communing.

30. **beads:** rosary; i.e., prayers.

31. **alderliefest:** most dear; dear beyond all others.

33. **ruder:** less courtly; **wit affords:** wisdom provides.

34. **minister:** supply.

36. **y-clad:** clothed.

39. **cheerful:** warmly welcoming.

43. **so:** if.

47. **imprimis:** in the first place.

The happiest gift that ever marquess gave,
The fairest queen that ever king received.

   King. Suffolk, arise. Welcome, Queen Margaret.
I can express no kinder sign of love   20
Than this kind kiss. O Lord, that lends me life,
Lend me a heart replete with thankfulness!
For Thou hast given me in this beauteous face
A world of earthly blessings to my soul,
If sympathy of love unite our thoughts.   25

   Queen. Great King of England and my gracious
     lord,
The mutual conference that my mind hath had,
By day, by night, waking and in my dreams,
In courtly company or at my beads,   30
With you, mine alderliefest sovereign,
Makes me the bolder to salute my king
With ruder terms, such as my wit affords
And overjoy of heart doth minister.

   King. Her sight did ravish; but her grace in speech, 35
Her words y-clad with wisdom's majesty,
Makes me from wond'ring fall to weeping joys,
Such is the fullness of my heart's content.
Lords, with one cheerful voice welcome my love.

   All. [*Kneeling*] Long live Queen Margaret, Eng- 40
     land's happiness!

   Queen. We thank you all.   *Flourish.*

   Suf. My Lord Protector, so it please your Grace,
Here are the articles of contracted peace
Between our sovereign and the French King Charles, 45
For eighteen months concluded by consent.

   Glou. [*Reads*] "Imprimis, It is agreed between the

58. **qualm:** literally, a sick feeling.

64. **of:** at; **proper:** personal.

68. **Duke of Suffolk:** the title was not actually bestowed until 1448, two years after Suffolk escorted Margaret to England.

71. **eighteen months:** the term of the truce.

76. **entertainment to:** welcome of.

Reignier, Duke of Anjou. From *Chronologie et sommaire des souverains* (1622).

French King Charles and William de la Pole, Marquess of Suffolk, ambassador for Henry King of England, that the said Henry shall espouse the Lady   50
Margaret, daughter unto Reignier King of Naples,
Sicilia, and Jerusalem, and crown her Queen of England ere the thirtieth of May next ensuing. Item, that
the Duchy of Anjou and the County of Maine shall
be released and delivered to the King her father—"   55
                         [*Lets the paper fall.*]

   King. Uncle, how now!
   Glou.   Pardon me, gracious lord:
Some sudden qualm hath struck me at the heart
And dimmed mine eyes, that I can read no further.
   King. Uncle of Winchester, I pray, read on.   60
   Car. [*Reads*] "Item, It is further agreed between
them that the Duchies of Anjou and Maine shall be
released and delivered over to the King her father,
and she sent over of the King of England's own proper
cost and charges, without having any dowry."   65
   King. They please us well. Lord Marquess, kneel
     down:
We here create thee the first Duke of Suffolk
And girt thee with the sword. Cousin of York,
We here discharge your Grace from being regent   70
I' the parts of France till term of eighteen months
Be full expired. Thanks, uncle Winchester,
Gloucester, York, Buckingham, Somerset,
Salisbury, and Warwick;
We thank you all for this great favor done,   75
In entertainment to my princely queen.
Come, let us in and with all speed provide

79. **peers . . . pillars:** Shakespeare characteristically puns on peers/piers (pillars).

83. **valor:** includes his general worthiness or value, as well as bravery.

88. **policy:** statesmanship.

97. **hath:** possibly a mistake for "had."

105. **Razing the characters:** scratching out the written records.

106. **monuments:** memorials.

107. **as:** as if.

To see her coronation be performed.
                    Exeunt King, Queen, and Suffolk.
  Glou. Brave peers of England, pillars of the state,
To you Duke Humphrey must unload his grief,   80
Your grief, the common grief of all the land.
What! did my brother Henry spend his youth,
His valor, coin, and people, in the wars?
Did he so often lodge in open field,
In winter's cold and summer's parching heat,   85
To conquer France, his true inheritance?
And did my brother Bedford toil his wits
To keep by policy what Henry got?
Have you yourselves, Somerset, Buckingham,
Brave York, Salisbury, and victorious Warwick,   90
Received deep scars in France and Normandy?
Or hath mine uncle Beaufort and myself,
With all the learned Council of the realm,
Studied so long, sat in the council house
Early and late, debating to and fro   95
How France and Frenchmen might be kept in awe,
And hath His Highness in his infancy
Crowned in Paris in despite of foes?
And shall these labors and these honors die?
Shall Henry's conquest, Bedford's vigilance,   100
Your deeds of war, and all our counsel die?
O peers of England, shameful is this league!
Fatal this marriage, canceling your fame,
Blotting your names from books of memory,
Razing the characters of your renown,   105
Defacing monuments of conquered France,
Undoing all, as all had never been!

110. **circumstance:** detail.

111. **For:** as for.

114. **rules the roast:** is master; the one who ruled the roast had the disposition of the choice parts of the meat. The modern phrase "rule the roost" is a corruption.

116. **large style:** long string of titles (Duke of Anjou, Lorraine, and Bar; King of Naples, Sicily, and Jerusalem); despite them, he actually possessed little land.

124. **myself did win them both:** Shakespeare attributes to Richard Neville the deeds of his father-in-law, Richard Beauchamp, Earl of Warwick, who died in 1439. Neville married Beauchamp's daughter Anne and through her succeeded to the title in 1449/50.

137. **proper:** fine; handsome (ironic).

138. **fifteenth:** a tax of one fifteenth on personal property. Hall's Chronicle is the source for this; in the last scene of *1 Henry VI* the King directs Suffolk to collect a tenth for his expenses.

Car. Nephew, what means this passionate discourse,
This peroration with such circumstance?   110
For France, 'tis ours, and we will keep it still.

Glou. Ay, uncle, we will keep it, if we can;
But now it is impossible we should.
Suffolk, the new-made Duke that rules the roast,
Hath given the Duchy of Anjou and Maine   115
Unto the poor King Reignier, whose large style
Agrees not with the leanness of his purse.

Sal. Now, by the death of Him that died for all,
These counties were the keys of Normandy.
But wherefore weeps Warwick, my valiant son?   120

War. For grief that they are past recovery:
For, were there hope to conquer them again,
My sword should shed hot blood, mine eyes no tears.
Anjou and Maine! myself did win them both;
Those provinces these arms of mine did conquer.   125
And are the cities that I got with wounds
Delivered up again with peaceful words?
Mort Dieu!

York. For Suffolk's Duke, may he be suffocate,
That dims the honor of this warlike isle!   130
France should have torn and rent my very heart
Before I would have yielded to this league.
I never read but England's kings have had
Large sums of gold and dowries with their wives;
And our King Henry gives away his own,   135
To match with her that brings no vantages.

Glou. A proper jest, and never heard before,
That Suffolk should demand a whole fifteenth

157. next of blood: nearest to the King in his claim to the throne by right of birth.

162. smoothing: ingratiating; polished.

A cardinal. From Hartmann Schopper, *Panoplia omnium il-liberalium* (1568).

For costs and charges in transporting her!
She should have stayed in France and starved in 140
    France,
Before—
    Car. My lord of Gloucester, now ye grow too hot:
It was the pleasure of my lord the King.
    Glou. My lord of Winchester, I know your mind: 145
'Tis not my speeches that you do mislike,
But 'tis my presence that doth trouble ye.
Rancor will out: proud prelate, in thy face
I see thy fury. If I longer stay
We shall begin our ancient bickerings.   150
Lordings, farewell; and say, when I am gone,
I prophesied France will be lost ere long.   *Exit.*
    Car. So, there goes our Protector in a rage.
'Tis known to you he is mine enemy,
Nay, more, an enemy unto you all,   155
And no great friend, I fear me, to the King.
Consider, lords, he is the next of blood
And heir apparent to the English crown.
Had Henry got an empire by his marriage,
And all the wealthy kingdoms of the West,   160
There's reason he should be displeased at it.
Look to it, lords; let not his smoothing words
Bewitch your hearts; be wise and circumspect.
What though the common people favor him,
Calling him "Humphrey, the good Duke of Glouces- 165
    ter,"
Clapping their hands and crying with loud voice,
"Jesu maintain your royal excellence!"
With "God preserve the good Duke Humphrey!"

170. **flattering gloss:** ability to put on a good show.

176. **hoise:** hoist; oust.

177. **brook:** stand.

178. **presently:** at once.

186. **Or:** either.

188. **Pride:** i.e., the Cardinal.

189. **preferment:** advancement.

190. **Behooves it us:** it is our responsibility.

192. **bear him:** behave.

195. **stout:** haughty; **as:** as if.

196. **demean:** conduct.

199. **plainness:** lack of pomp; **housekeeping:** hospitality. The nobility were expected to be generous to those less fortunate.

I fear me, lords, for all this flattering gloss,   170
He will be found a dangerous Protector.

 Buck. Why should he, then, protect our sovereign,
He being of age to govern of himself?
Cousin of Somerset, join you with me,
And all together, with the Duke of Suffolk,   175
We'll quickly hoise Duke Humphrey from his seat.

 Car. This weighty business will not brook delay;
I'll to the Duke of Suffolk presently.   *Exit.*

 Som. Cousin of Buckingham, though Humphrey's
  pride   180
And greatness of his place be grief to us,
Yet let us watch the haughty Cardinal:
His insolence is more intolerable
Than all the princes in the land beside.
If Gloucester be displaced, he'll be Protector.   185

 Buck. Or thou or I, Somerset, will be Protector,
Despite Duke Humphrey or the Cardinal.
     Exeunt Buckingham and Somerset.

 Sal. Pride went before, ambition follows him.
While these do labor for their own preferment,
Behooves it us to labor for the realm.   190
I never saw but Humphrey Duke of Gloucester
Did bear him like a noble gentleman.
Oft have I seen the haughty Cardinal,
More like a soldier than a man o' the church,
As stout and proud as he were lord of all,   195
Swear like a ruffian and demean himself
Unlike the ruler of a commonweal.
Warwick, my son, the comfort of my age,
Thy deeds, thy plainness, and thy housekeeping

200. **commons:** common people; multitude.

202. **brother York:** York was married to Salisbury's sister, Cicely Neville.

211. **cherish:** foster.

212. **tend:** tend toward; look after.

218. **main:** main problem; the country's welfare.

226. **Stands on a tickle point:** is insecure.

227. **Suffolk concluded:** the return of Anjou and Maine was not agreed upon as part of the marriage treaty, although the French raised the question. It was the King who later yielded to French pressure for their return.

Hath won the greatest favor of the commons,   200
Excepting none but good Duke Humphrey.
And, brother York, thy acts in Ireland,
In bringing them to civil discipline,
Thy late exploits done in the heart of France,
When thou wert regent for our sovereign,   205
Have made thee feared and honored of the people.
Join we together, for the public good,
In what we can to bridle and suppress
The pride of Suffolk and the Cardinal,
With Somerset's and Buckingham's ambition;   210
And, as we may, cherish Duke Humphrey's deeds,
While they do tend the profit of the land.

    War. So God help Warwick as he loves the land
And common profit of his country!

      York. [*Aside*] And so says York, for he hath greatest 215
      cause.

      Sal. Then let's make haste away and look unto the
      main.

    War. Unto the main! O father, Maine is lost;
That Maine which by main force Warwick did win   220
And would have kept so long as breath did last!
Main chance, father, you meant; but I meant Maine,
Which I will win from France or else be slain.
                       Exeunt Warwick and Salisbury.

    York. Anjou and Maine are given to the French;
Paris is lost; the state of Normandy   225
Stands on a tickle point, now they are gone.
Suffolk concluded on the articles;
The peers agreed; and Henry was well pleased
To change two dukedoms for a duke's fair daughter.

232. **make cheap pennyworths of:** value little; give away.

235. **silly:** helpless.

236. **hapless:** unlucky.

244. **Althaea:** the Queen of Calydon. When her son, Meleager, was born the Fates threw a log on the fire and warned her that he would live only until it was consumed. She snatched it up, doused the flame, and preserved it, but when Meleager killed her brothers, she set the log aflame and her son was destroyed as it burned.

245. **Prince's heart:** heart of the Prince.

255. **childish:** Henry was twenty-five by now, but Shakespeare preferred to exaggerate his immaturity.

Althaea burning the brand on which Meleager's life depended. From Gabriele Simeoni, *La vita et Metamorfoseo d'Ovidio* (1559).

I cannot blame them all: what is't to them? 230
'Tis thine they give away and not their own.
Pirates may make cheap pennyworths of their pillage,
And purchase friends and give to courtesans,
Still reveling like lords till all be gone;
Whileas the silly owner of the goods 235
Weeps over them and wrings his hapless hands,
And shakes his head and trembling stands aloof,
While all is shared and all is borne away,
Ready to starve and dare not touch his own.
So York must sit and fret and bite his tongue, 240
While his own lands are bargained for and sold.
Methinks the realms of England, France, and Ireland
Bear that proportion to my flesh and blood
As did the fatal brand Althaea burned
Unto the Prince's heart of Calydon. 245
Anjou and Maine both given unto the French!
Cold news for me, for I had hope of France,
Even as I have of fertile England's soil.
A day will come when York shall claim his own;
And therefore I will take the Nevilles' parts 250
And make a show of love to proud Duke Humphrey,
And, when I spy advantage, claim the crown,
For that's the golden mark I seek to hit.
Nor shall proud Lancaster usurp my right,
Nor hold the scepter in his childish fist, 255
Nor wear the diadem upon his head,
Whose church-like humors fits not for a crown.
Then, York, be still awhile, till time do serve.
Watch thou and wake when others be asleep,
To pry into the secrets of the state; 260

263. **at jars:** into conflict.
268. **force perforce:** forcibly, against his will.

IIIIIIIIIIIIIIIIIIIIIIIIIIIIIIIIIIIIIIIIIIIII

I.[ii.] Gloucester relates to his wife a puzzling dream: the breaking of his staff of office and the placing of the heads of Somerset and Suffolk on the two pieces. The Duchess interprets this as symbolic of his greatness and power. She in turn tells him that she has dreamed of being seated in the coronation chair at Westminster Abbey, where King Henry and Queen Margaret knelt to her and placed a crown on her head. Gloucester, shocked, scolds her for such audacious thoughts. A messenger summons them to ride to St. Albans, where the King and Queen are to hawk. The Duchess promises Gloucester to follow shortly, but in an aside she expresses her discontent that she must follow rather than lead. She confers with a priest about a meeting with Margery Jourdain, a witch, and Roger Bolingbroke, a conjurer, whom she wishes to question about the future. The priest, John Hume, assures her that arrangements have been made but reveals to the audience that he is in the pay of the Cardinal and the Duke of Suffolk, who hope to use the Duchess' ambition to damage Gloucester.

IIIIIIIIIIIIIIIIIIIIIIIIIIIIIIIIIII

2. **Ceres:** Italian goddess of agriculture and fertility.
4. **favors:** looks.
5. **sullen:** dull.
8. **Enchased:** engraved.

10

Till Henry, surfeiting in joys of love,
With his new bride and England's dear-bought Queen,
And Humphrey with the peers be fall'n at jars.
Then will I raise aloft the milk-white rose,
With whose sweet smell the air shall be perfumed,   265
And in my standard bear the arms of York,
To grapple with the house of Lancaster;
And, force perforce, I'll make him yield the crown,
Whose bookish rule hath pulled fair England down.

                                       Exit.

[Scene II. The Duke of Gloucester's house.]

Enter Duke Humphrey and his wife, Eleanor.

  Duch. Why droops my lord, like overripened corn,
Hanging the head at Ceres' plenteous load?
Why doth the great Duke Humphrey knit his brows,
As frowning at the favors of the world?
Why are thine eyes fixed to the sullen earth,   5
Gazing on that which seems to dim thy sight?
What seest thou there? King Henry's diadem,
Enchased with all the honors of the world?
If so, gaze on, and grovel on thy face,
Until thy head be circled with the same.   10
Put forth thy hand, reach at the glorious gold.
What, is't too short? I'll lengthen it with mine;
And, having both together heaved it up,
We'll both together lift our heads to Heaven
And never more abase our sight so low   15

16. **vouchsafe:** condescend.

22. **sad:** grave.

24. **requite:** repay.

25. **rehearsal:** relation.

26. **staff:** a baton that symbolized his authority.

34. **argument:** token.

35–6. he that breaks a stick of Gloucester's grove/ Shall lose his head for his presumption: this is reminiscent of the story of the grove sacred to Diana at Lake Nemi, the theme of Sir James Frazer's *The Golden Bough.*

44. **chide:** scold.

45. **ill-nurtured:** ill-bred; indecorous.

The drooping heads of overripened corn (wheat). From Geoffrey Whitney, *A Choice of Emblems* (1586).

As to vouchsafe one glance unto the ground.

 Glou. O Nell, sweet Nell, if thou dost love thy lord,
Banish the canker of ambitious thoughts.
And may that thought, when I imagine ill
Against my king and nephew, virtuous Henry, 20
Be my last breathing in this mortal world!
My troublous dreams this night doth make me sad.

 Duch. What dreamed my lord? Tell me, and I'll
  requite it
With sweet rehearsal of my morning's dream. 25

 Glou. Methought this staff, mine office badge in
  court,
Was broke in twain; by whom I have forgot,
But, as I think, it was by the Cardinal;
And on the pieces of the broken wand 30
Were placed the heads of Edmund Duke of Somerset
And William de la Pole, first Duke of Suffolk.
This was my dream: what it doth bode, God knows.

 Duch. Tut, this was nothing but an argument
That he that breaks a stick of Gloucester's grove 35
Shall lose his head for his presumption.
But list to me, my Humphrey, my sweet duke:
Methought I sat in seat of majesty,
In the cathedral church of Westminster,
And in that chair where kings and queens were 40
  crowned;
Where Henry and Dame Margaret kneeled to me,
And on my head did set the diadem.

 Glou. Nay, Eleanor, then must I chide outright:
Presumptuous dame, ill-nurtured Eleanor, 45
Art thou not second woman in the realm,

49. **compass:** synonymous with **reach.**
50. **hammering:** cudgeling the brain to plot.
54. **choleric:** angry.
57. **checked:** corrected.
62. **Whereas:** where.
65. **Follow I must: I cannot go before:** proverbial. Eleanor means that she would be pre-eminent in the realm if she could but is forced to endure a humbler role.
72. **Sir John:** the title is the English form of the Latin *dominus,* indicating that he is a member of the clergy and a Master of Arts.

And the Protector's wife, beloved of him?
Hast thou not worldly pleasure at command,
Above the reach or compass of thy thought?
And wilt thou still be hammering treachery,   50
To tumble down thy husband and thyself
From top of honor to disgrace's feet?
Away from me, and let me hear no more!
  Duch. What, what, my lord! are you so choleric
With Eleanor for telling but her dream?   55
Next time I'll keep my dreams unto myself
And not be checked.
  Glou. Nay, be not angry: I am pleased again.

Enter Messenger.

  Mess. My Lord Protector, 'tis His Highness'
    pleasure   60
You do prepare to ride unto St. Albans,
Whereas the King and Queen do mean to hawk.
  Glou. I go. Come, Nell, thou wilt ride with us?
  Duch. Yes, my good lord, I'll follow presently.
              Exeunt Gloucester [and Messenger].
Follow I must: I cannot go before,   65
While Gloucester bears this base and humble mind.
Were I a man, a duke, and next of blood,
I would remove these tedious stumbling-blocks
And smooth my way upon their headless necks;
And, being a woman, I will not be slack   70
To play my part in Fortune's pageant.
Where are you there? Sir John! nay, fear not, man,
We are alone: here's none but thee and I.

75. **but Grace:** entitled only to be called "your Grace," the proper form of polite address to a Duchess.

87. **propounded:** posed.

95. **Marry, and shall:** indeed I shall. **Marry** is an interjection shortened from "by the Virgin Mary."

96. **no words but mum:** a proverbial warning to be discreet.

100. **flies:** comes swiftly; **coast:** part of the world; source.

Enter Hume.

Hume. Jesus preserve your royal Majesty!
Duch. What sayst thou? Majesty! I am but Grace.   75
Hume. But, by the grace of God and Hume's advice,
Your Grace's title shall be multiplied.
   Duch. What sayst thou, man? Hast thou as yet con-
      ferred
With Margery Jourdain, the cunning witch,   80
With Roger Bolingbroke, the conjurer?
And will they undertake to do me good?
   Hume. This they have promised, to show your
      Highness
A spirit raised from depth of underground,   85
That shall make answer to such questions
As by your Grace shall be propounded him.
   Duch. It is enough: I'll think upon the questions.
When from St. Albans we do make return,
We'll see these things effected to the full.   90
Here, Hume, take this reward: make merry, man,
With thy confederates in this weighty cause.   *Exit.*
   Hume. Hume must make merry with the Duchess'
      gold;
Marry, and shall. But, how now, Sir John Hume!   95
Seal up your lips and give no words but mum.
The business asketh silent secrecy.
Dame Eleanor gives gold to bring the witch;
Gold cannot come amiss, were she a devil.
Yet have I gold flies from another coast;   100
I dare not say, from the rich Cardinal

107. **broker:** go-between.

112. **wrack:** ruin.

113. **attainture:** taint; disgrace; or possibly "attainder," conviction for treason.

114. **Sort how it will:** however it ends.

▪▪▪▪▪▪▪▪▪▪▪▪▪▪▪▪▪▪▪▪▪▪▪▪▪▪▪▪▪▪▪▪▪▪▪▪

I.[iii.] Suffolk and the Queen, intercepting petitions intended for Gloucester, resent this evidence of the Protector's power. A petition of an armorer's man, charging his master with calling York the rightful King of England, provides evidence against the ambitious Duke. The Queen reveals her disappointment in the King and her resentment of his Council and of Gloucester's haughty wife. Suffolk explains that he has set a trap for the Duchess which may also rid them of the Protector. While Gloucester holds power, they must ally themselves with the Cardinal and other nobles. At a Council meeting, the King will not choose between York and Somerset for the new Regent of France. Gloucester's enemies declare that the King no longer needs a Protector, and Gloucester leaves in a rage. When his anger has cooled, Gloucester proposes York for Regent. Suffolk has the armorer and his man brought in. Since York's name is involved in a charge of treason, Gloucester rules that Somerset should be sent to France. He proposes a combat between the armorer and his man to determine the truth of the charges.

▪▪▪▪▪▪▪▪▪▪▪▪▪▪▪▪▪▪▪▪▪▪▪▪▪▪▪▪▪▪

3. **in the quill:** in a body; but the origin of the word in this sense is uncertain.

6. **'a:** he.

14

And from the great and new-made Duke of Suffolk,
Yet I do find it so; for, to be plain,
They, knowing Dame Eleanor's aspiring humor,
Have hired me to undermine the Duchess   105
And buzz these conjurations in her brain.
They say, "A crafty knave does need no broker";
Yet am I Suffolk and the Cardinal's broker.
Hume, if you take not heed, you shall go near
To call them both a pair of crafty knaves.   110
Well, so it stands; and thus, I fear, at last
Hume's knavery will be the Duchess' wrack,
And her attainture will be Humphrey's fall.
Sort how it will, I shall have gold for all.

Exit.

[Scene III. London. The palace.]

Enter three or four Petitioners, [Peter,] the Armorer's man, being one.

   1. Pet. My masters, let's stand close. My Lord Protector will come this way by and by, and then we may deliver our supplications in the quill.
   2. Pet. Marry, the Lord protect him, for he's a good man! Jesu bless him!   ᵗ

Enter Suffolk and Queen.

   Peter. Here 'a comes, methinks, and the Queen with him. I'll be the first, sure.

16. **and't please:** if it please.
21. **commons:** common lands.
33. **pursuivant:** a royal messenger empowered to make arrests.
33–4. **presently:** immediately.

2. Pet. Come back, fool: this is the Duke of Suffolk, and not my Lord Protector.

Suf. How now, fellow! wouldst anything with me? 1(

1. Pet. I pray, my lord, pardon me: I took ye for my Lord Protector.

Queen. [*Reading*] "To my Lord Protector!" Are your supplications to His Lordship? Let me see them: what is thine? 1!

1. Pet. Mine is, and't please your Grace, against John Goodman, my lord Cardinal's man, for keeping my house and lands and wife and all from me.

Suf. Thy wife too! That's some wrong, indeed. What's yours? What's here! [*Reads*] "Against the 2(Duke of Suffolk, for enclosing the commons of Melford." How now, sir knave!

2. Pet. Alas, sir, I am but a poor petitioner of our whole township.

Peter. [*Giving his petition*] Against my master, 2! Thomas Horner, for saying that the Duke of York was rightful heir to the crown.

Queen. What sayst thou? Did the Duke of York say he was rightful heir to the crown?

Peter. That my master was? No, forsooth: my mas- 3(ter said that he was, and that the King was an usurper.

Suf. Who is there? (*Enter Servant.*) Take this fellow in, and send for his master with a pursuivant presently. We'll hear more of your matter before the King.
                              Exit [*Servant with Peter*].

Queen. And as for you, that love to be protected 3! Under the wings of our Protector's grace,

38. **cullions:** contemptible wretches.

43. **Albion:** ancient, mainly poetic, name for Great Britain.

44. **still:** ever.

46. **style:** synonymous with **title.**

52. **courtship:** courtliness; **proportion:** physical attributes.

55. **His champions:** those to whom he looks for protection. Queen Elizabeth had an official Champion who took part in tournaments.

A knight armored for the tilt. From Conrad Lycosthenes, *Prodigiorum liber* (1557).

Begin your suits anew, and sue to him.
                          Tears the supplications.
Away, base cullions! Suffolk, let them go.
    All. Come, let's be gone.   *Exeunt.*
    Queen. My Lord of Suffolk, say, is this the guise,   40
Is this the fashion in the court of England?
Is this the government of Britain's isle
And this the royalty of Albion's king?
What, shall King Henry be a pupil still
Under the surly Gloucester's governance?   45
Am I a queen in title and in style,
And must be made a subject to a duke?
I tell thee, Pole, when in the city Tours
Thou ranst a tilt in honor of my love,
And stolest away the ladies' hearts of France,   50
I thought King Henry had resembled thee
In courage, courtship, and proportion:
But all his mind is bent to holiness,
To number Ave Maries on his beads;
His champions are the prophets and apostles,   55
His weapons holy saws of sacred writ,
His study is his tiltyard, and his loves
Are brazen images of canonized saints.
I would the college of the cardinals
Would choose him Pope and carry him to Rome,   60
And set the triple crown upon his head:
That were a state fit for his holiness.
    Suf. Madam, be patient: as I was cause
Your Highness came to England, so will I
In England work your Grace's full content.   65

82. **Contemptuous:** contemptible; **callet:** hussy.

83. **vaunted:** boasted; **minions:** favorites.

87. **limed a bush:** i.e., laid a trap. A sticky substance called "birdlime" was spread on bushes to trap small birds. Decoys were sometimes used to attract the birds to the bush.

88. **choir:** company, with a pun.

89. **lays:** songs.

91. **let her rest:** forget her.

96. **late complaint:** Peter's petition against Horner.

Queen. Beside the haughty Protector, have we
    Beaufort,
The imperious churchman, Somerset, Buckingham,
And grumbling York; and not the least of these
But can do more in England than the King.   70

Suf. And he of these that can do most of all
Cannot do more in England than the Nevilles:
Salisbury and Warwick are no simple peers.

Queen. Not all these lords do vex me half so much
As that proud dame the Lord Protector's wife.   75
She sweeps it through the court with troops of ladies,
More like an empress than Duke Humphrey's wife.
Strangers in court do take her for the Queen:
She bears a duke's revenues on her back,
And in her heart she scorns our poverty.   80
Shall I not live to be avenged on her?
Contemptuous base-born callet as she is,
She vaunted 'mongst her minions t' other day,
The very train of her worst wearing gown
Was better worth than all my father's lands,   85
Till Suffolk gave two dukedoms for his daughter.

Suf. Madam, myself have limed a bush for her
And placed a choir of such enticing birds
That she will light to listen to the lays
And never mount to trouble you again.   90
So, let her rest: and, madam, list to me;
For I am bold to counsel you in this.
Although we fancy not the Cardinal,
Yet must we join with him and with the lords,
Till we have brought Duke Humphrey in disgrace.   95
As for the Duke of York, this late complaint

Ent. 99. **Sennet:** a traditional set of notes played on the trumpet to announce the arrival of a great person.

101. **Or:** either.

102. **ill demeaned himself:** conducted himself badly.

103. **denayed:** denied.

114. **forsooth:** indeed.

116. **censure:** judgment; opinion.

Will make but little for his benefit.
So, one by one, we'll weed them all at last,
And you yourself shall steer the happy helm.

Sound a Sennet. Enter the King, Duke Humphrey,
Cardinal, Buckingham, York, [Somerset,] Salisbury,
Warwick, and the Duchess [of Gloucester].

King. For my part, noble lords, I care not which: 100
Or Somerset or York, all's one to me.
    York. If York have ill demeaned himself in France,
Then let him be denayed the regentship.
    Som. If Somerset be unworthy of the place,
Let York be Regent: I will yield to him. 105
    War. Whether your Grace be worthy, yea or no,
Dispute not that: York is the worthier.
    Car. Ambitious Warwick, let thy betters speak.
    War. The Cardinal's not my better in the field.
    Buck. All in this presence are thy betters, Warwick. 110
    War. Warwick may live to be the best of all.
    Sal. Peace, son! and show some reason, Buckingham,
Why Somerset should be preferred in this.
    Queen. Because the King, forsooth, will have it so.
    Glou. Madam, the King is old enough himself 115
To give his censure: these are no women's matters.
    Queen. If he be old enough, what needs your Grace
To be Protector of His Excellence?
    Glou. Madam, I am Protector of the realm
And at his pleasure will resign my place. 120
    Suf. Resign it then and leave thine insolence.
Since thou wert King—as who is King but thou?—

126. **bondmen:** slaves.

127. **racked:** plundered (by taxation).

136. **suspect:** suspicion.

139. **cry you mercy:** beg your pardon.

142. **Ten Commandments:** i.e., scratches from the nails of her ten fingers. This proverbial identification of the fingers with the Ten Commandments may derive from a habit of reciting the Commandments and keeping count of their number on the fingers.

143. **against her will:** unintentional.

146. **most master wear no breeches:** the boss does not wear the breeches; a proverbial way of saying that the wife rules the household.

150. **tickled:** stirred up; **fume:** anger.

The commonwealth hath daily run to wrack;
The Dauphin hath prevailed beyond the seas;
And all the peers and nobles of the realm   125
Have been as bondmen to thy sovereignty.

   Car. The commons hast thou racked; the clergy's
     bags
Are lank and lean with thy extortions.

   Som. Thy sumptuous buildings and thy wife's attire 130
Have cost a mass of public treasury.

   Buck. Thy cruelty in execution
Upon offenders hath exceeded law
And left thee to the mercy of the law.

   Queen. Thy sale of offices and towns in France,   135
If they were known, as the suspect is great,
Would make thee quickly hop without thy head.

        Exit Gloucester. [The Queen drops her fan.]
Give me my fan! What, minion! can ye not?
        She gives the Duchess a box on the ear.
I cry you mercy, madam: was it you?

   Duch. Was't I! yea, I it was, proud Frenchwoman.   140
Could I come near your beauty with my nails,
I'd set my Ten Commandments in your face.

   King. Sweet aunt, be quiet; 'twas against her will.

   Duch. Against her will! good king, look to 't in time;
She'll hamper thee and dandle thee like a baby.   145
Though in this place most master wear no breeches,
She shall not strike Dame Eleanor unrevenged. *Exit.*

   Buck. Lord Cardinal, I will follow Eleanor
And listen after Humphrey, how he proceeds.
She's tickled now; her fume needs no spurs,   150
She'll gallop far enough to her destruction. *Exit.*

Enter Gloucester.

Glou. Now, lords, my choler being overblown
With walking once about the quadrangle,
I come to talk of commonwealth affairs.
As for your spiteful, false objections,   15
Prove them and I lie open to the law:
But God in mercy so deal with my soul
As I in duty love my king and country!
But, to the matter that we have in hand:
I say, my sovereign, York is meetest man   16
To be your regent in the realm of France.

Suf. Before we make election, give me leave
To show some reason, of no little force,
That York is most unmeet of any man.

York. I'll tell thee, Suffolk, why I am unmeet: 16
First, for I cannot flatter thee in pride;
Next, if I be appointed for the place,
My Lord of Somerset will keep me here,
Without discharge, money, or furniture,
Till France be won into the Dauphin's hands.   17
Last time, I danced attendance on his will
Till Paris was besieged, famished, and lost.

War. That can I witness; and a fouler fact
Did never traitor in the land commit.

Suf. Peace, headstrong Warwick!   17

War. Image of pride, why should I hold my peace?

182. **Please it:** if it please.

194. **mechanical:** a contemptuous term for a craftsman, one who works with his hands.

Armorer at work. From Hartmann Schopper, *Panoplia omnium illiberalium* (1568).

*Enter [Horner] the Armorer, and his man [Peter,
                    guarded].*

   Suf. Because here is a man accused of treason.
Pray God the Duke of York excuse himself!
   York. Doth anyone accuse York for a traitor?
   King. What meanst thou, Suffolk? Tell me, what are   180
     these?
   Suf. Please it your Majesty, this is the man
That doth accuse his master of high treason.
His words were these: that Richard Duke of York
Was rightful heir unto the English crown,   185
And that your Majesty was an usurper.
   King. Say, man, were these thy words?
   Horn. And't shall please your Majesty, I never said
nor thought any such matter. God is my witness, I
am falsely accused by the villain.   190
   Peter. By these ten bones, my lords, he did speak
them to me in the garret one night, as we were scour-
ing my lord of York's armor.
   York. Base dunghill villain and mechanical,
I'll have thy head for this thy traitor's speech.   195
I do beseech your royal Majesty,
Let him have all the rigor of the law.
   Horn. Alas, my lord, hang me, if ever I spake the
words. My accuser is my 'prentice; and when I did
correct him for his fault the other day, he did vow   200
upon his knees he would be even with me. I have
good witness of this: therefore I beseech your Maj-

213–14. [King . . . French]: added from the Quarto, since the King's approval seems necessary and the Folio gives him nothing to say.

esty, do not cast away an honest man for a villain's
accusation.

King. Uncle, what shall we say to this in law? 205

Glou. This doom, my lord, if I may judge:
Let Somerset be regent o'er the French,
Because in York this breeds suspicion.
And let these have a day appointed them
For single combat in convenient place, 210
For he hath witness of his servant's malice.
This is the law and this Duke Humphrey's doom.

[*King.* Then be it so, my lord of Somerset:
We make your Grace regent over the French.]

Som. I humbly thank your royal Majesty. 215

Horn. And I accept the combat willingly.

Peter. Alas, my lord, I cannot fight; for God's sake,
pity my case. The spite of man prevaileth against me.
O Lord, have mercy upon me! I shall never be able
to fight a blow. O Lord, my heart! 220

Glou. Sirrah, or you must fight, or else be hanged.

King. Away with them to prison; and the day of
combat shall be the last of the next month. Come,
Somerset, we'll see thee sent away.

Flourish. Exeunt.

I.[iv.] Hume and another priest bring Margery Jourdain and Roger Bolingbroke to the garden of Gloucester's house. The Duchess' questions about the fates of King Henry, Suffolk, and Somerset are put to a spirit raised by conjuration, which answers in riddling fashion. York and Buckingham break in and arrest the party. York confiscates the questions and answers and agrees that Buckingham should ride to St. Albans to tell Gloucester and the King about the matter. He also dispatches a servant to invite Salisbury and Warwick to sup with him.

▐▐▐▐▐▐▐▐▐▐▐▐▐▐▐▐▐▐▐▐▐▐▐▐▐▐▐▐

7. **convenient:** appropriate.
13. **Well said:** well done; greetings.
14. **gear:** business.
18. **bandogs:** watch dogs.

[Scene IV. Gloucester's garden.]

Enter [Margery Jourdain,] the Witch, two Priests,
  [Hume and Southwell,] and Bolingbroke.

Hume. Come, my masters: the Duchess, I tell you,
expects performance of your promises.

Bol. Master Hume, we are therefor provided.
Will Her Ladyship behold and hear our exorcisms?

Hume. Ay, what else? Fear you not her courage.   5

Bol. I have heard her reported to be a woman of an
invincible spirit: but it shall be convenient, Master
Hume, that you be by her aloft, while we be busy
below; and so, I pray you, go, in God's name, and
leave us. (*Exit Hume.*) Mother Jourdain, be you pros-   10
trate and grovel on the earth; John Southwell, read
you; and let us to our work.

Enter Duchess aloft, [Hume following].

Duch. Well said, my masters; and welcome all.
To this gear the sooner the better.

Bol. Patience, good lady: wizards know their times.   15
Deep night, dark night, the silent of the night,
The time of night when Troy was set on fire;
The time when screech owls cry, and bandogs howl,
And spirits walk, and ghosts break up their graves,
That time best fits the work we have in hand.   20

22. **fast:** secure; **verge:** confine.

23. **Adsum:** I am here.

24. **Asmath:** a made-up name for a fiend.

28. **That:** would that; **said and done:** finished speaking.

41. **avoid:** be gone.

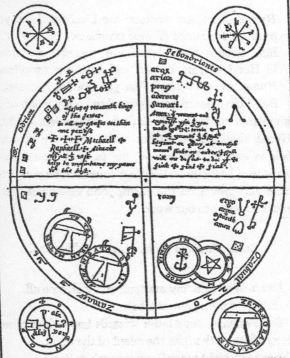

A circle for conjuring. From "The Book of Magic" (ca. 1580). (Folger MS. V.b.26.)

Madam, sit you and fear not: whom we raise,
We will make fast within a hallowed verge.

*Here do the ceremonies belonging, and make the
circle. Bolingbroke or Southwell reads, Conjuro te,
etc. It thunders and lightens terribly: then the Spirit
riseth.*

 Spir. Adsum.
 M. *Jour.* Asmath,
By the eternal God, Whose name and power   25
Thou tremblest at, answer that I shall ask;
For, till thou speak, thou shalt not pass from hence.
 Spir. Ask what thou wilt. That I had said and done!
 Bol. [*Reads*] "First, of the King: what shall of him
  become?"   30
 Spir. The duke yet lives that Henry shall depose,
But him outlive and die a violent death.
 [*As the Spirit speaks, Southwell writes the answer.*]
 Bol. "What fates await the Duke of Suffolk?"
 Spir. By water shall he die and take his end.
 Bol. "What shall befall the Duke of Somerset?" 35
 Spir. Let him shun castles:
Safer shall he be upon the sandy plains
Than where castles mounted stand.
Have done, for more I hardly can endure.
 Bol. Descend to darkness and the burning lake! 40
False fiend, avoid! *Thunder and lightning. Exit Spirit.*

43. Beldam: witch; **at an inch:** closely; a proverbial phrase.

48. guerdoned: rewarded; **deserts:** merits. York speaks sarcastically.

49. Not half so bad as thine: i.e., my deserving is not half so bad as thine.

50. Injurious: insulting.

52. clapped up close: securely imprisoned.

55. trinkets: toys; the accessories to their conjuration; **forthcoming:** kept in readiness to be produced at the proper time.

65. Aio te . . . posse: "I tell you, son of Aeacus, you the Romans can conquer," the ambiguous answer made by the Pythian oracle to Pyrrhus when he sought advice before attacking Rome, according to Ennius, *Annales*.

*Enter the Duke of York and the Duke of Buckingham
with their Guard and break in.*

    York. Lay hands upon these traitors and their trash.
Beldam, I think we watched you at an inch.
What, madam, are you there? The King and common-
    weal   45
Are deeply indebted for this piece of pains.
My Lord Protector will, I doubt it not,
See you well guerdoned for these good deserts.
    Duch. Not half so bad as thine to England's king,
Injurious Duke, that threatest where's no cause.   50
    Buck. True, madam, none at all: what call you this?
Away with them! Let them be clapped up close,
And kept asunder. You, madam, shall with us.
Stafford, take her to thee.
        [*Exeunt, above, Duchess and Hume, guarded.*]
We'll see your trinkets here all forthcoming.   55
All, away!
        [*Exeunt guard with Jourdain, Southwell, etc.*]
    York. Lord Buckingham, methinks you watched her
    well:
A pretty plot, well chosen to build upon!
Now, pray, my lord, let's see the Devil's writ.   60
What have we here?
Reads.
"The duke yet lives that Henry shall depose,
But him outlive and die a violent death."
Why, this is just
Aio te, Aeacida, Romanos vincere posse.   65

69. **betide:** befall.

78. **these news:** news originally meant "new things," deriving from Old French *nouveles* and Latin *nova*.

83. **post:** speedy messenger.

Well, to the rest:
"Tell me, what fate awaits the Duke of Suffolk?
By water shall he die and take his end.
What shall betide the Duke of Somerset?
Let him shun castles: 70
Safer shall he be upon the sandy plains
Than where castles mounted stand."
Come, come, my lords.
These oracles are hardly attained
And hardly understood.   75
The King is now in progress toward St. Albans,
With him the husband of this lovely lady.
Thither goes these news, as fast as horse can carry
     them:
A sorry breakfast for my Lord Protector.   80
     Buck. Your Grace shall give me leave, my lord of
          York,
To be the post, in hope of his reward.
     York. At your pleasure, my good lord. Who's within
          there, ho!   85

Enter a Servingman.

Invite my lords of Salisbury and Warwick
To sup with me tomorrow night. Away!

                                              Exeunt.

THE SECOND PART
OF
HENRY THE SIXTH

ACT II

[II.i.] The royal party return from their hawking expedition. Gloucester and Cardinal Beaufort quarrel and secretly agree to fight a duel. The Mayor and townfolk of St. Albans bring in Saunder Simpcox, who claims to have been cured of lifelong blindness by St. Alban. Gloucester questions the fellow and reveals him as a sham. His moment of triumph is brief, however, because Buckingham then arrives with a report of the Duchess' conjuration and arrest. Gloucester sorrowfully states his determination to renounce his wife if she is guilty of trafficking with witches.

━━━━━━━━━━━━━━━━━━

1. **flying at the brook:** hawking for waterfowl, such as ducks.

2. **these seven years' day:** any day this last seven years.

3. **by your leave:** correct me if I am wrong.

4. **old Joan had not gone out:** i.e., the falcon named Joan would not have pursued the quarry; presumably **old Joan** would not have had the stamina to fly in a high wind.

5. **what a point . . . your falcon made:** what a strategic position your falcon reached.

6. **pitch:** height.

8. **fain of climbing high:** eager to fly high; ambitious. The King probably also has in mind aspirations to Heaven.

9. **and:** if; **like:** please.

10. **tower:** soar.

17–8. **How think you by that:** what do you think of that.

27

[ACT II]

[Scene I. St. Albans.]

*Enter the King, Queen, Gloucester, Cardinal, and
Suffolk, with Falconers halloing.*

Queen. Believe me, lords, for flying at the brook
I saw not better sport these seven years' day.
Yet, by your leave, the wind was very high;
And, ten to one, old Joan had not gone out.

King. But what a point, my lord, your falcon made, 5
And what a pitch she flew above the rest!
To see how God in all His creatures works!
Yea, man and birds are fain of climbing high.

Suf. No marvel, and it like your Majesty,
My Lord Protector's hawks do tower so well: 10
They know their master loves to be aloft
And bears his thoughts above his falcon's pitch.

Glou. My lord, 'tis but a base, ignoble mind
That mounts no higher than a bird can soar.

Car. I thought as much: he would be above the 15
clouds.

Glou. Ay, my lord Cardinal? How think you by
that?

27

24. **Pernicious:** destructive.

25. **smoothst it so:** so thoroughly deceives with false appearances.

27. **peremptory:** dogmatic; intolerant of different views.

28. **Tantaene animis caelestibus irae:** so much anger in heavenly souls? (Vergil, *Aeneid*, i.11).

40. **blessed are the peacemakers:** see Matt. 5:9.

41–2. **peace I make . . . with my sword:** compare Matt. 10:34: "I came not to send peace but a sword."

47–8. **Make up no factious numbers:** assemble no followers to support you.

49. **answer:** defend.

Were it not good your Grace could fly to Heaven?
  King. The treasury of everlasting joy.   20
  Car. Thy Heaven is on earth; thine eyes and
    thoughts
Beat on a crown, the treasure of thy heart;
Pernicious Protector, dangerous peer,
That smoothst it so with king and commonweal!   25
  Glou. What, Cardinal, is your priesthood grown
    peremptory?
Tantaene animis caelestibus irae?
Churchmen so hot? Good uncle, hide such malice;
With such holiness can you do it?   30
  Suf. No malice, sir; no more than well becomes
So good a quarrel and so bad a peer.
  Glou. As who, my lord?
  Suf.   Why, as you, my lord,
An't like your lordly Lord's Protectorship.   35
  Glou. Why, Suffolk, England knows thine insolence.
  Queen. And thy ambition, Gloucester.
  King.   I prithee, peace,
Good queen, and whet not on these furious peers,
For blessed are the peacemakers on earth.   40
  Car. Let me be blessed for the peace I make,
Against this proud Protector, with my sword!
  Glou. [*Aside to Cardinal*] Faith, holy uncle, would
    'twere come to that!
  Car. [*Aside to Gloucester*] Marry, when thou   45
    darest.
  Glou. [*Aside to Cardinal*] Make up no factious
    numbers for the matter;
In thine own person answer thy abuse.

57. **two-hand sword:** a sword so large that it had to be wielded with both hands.

59. **Are ye advised:** have you decided.

66. **fence:** knowledge of fencing technique.

67. **Medice, teipsum:** "physician, heal thyself," Latin rendering from the Vulgate of Luke 4:23.

69. **stomachs:** resentful tempers.

73. **compound this strife:** settle this quarrel.

Hawking. From Erasmo di Valvasone, *La caccia* (ca. 1602).

 Car. [*Aside to Gloucester*] Ay, where thou darest 50
  not peep: and if thou darest,
This evening, on the east side of the grove.
 King. How now, my lords!
 Car.   Believe me, cousin Gloucester,
Had not your man put up the fowl so suddenly, 55
We had had more sport. [*Aside to Gloucester*] Come
  with thy two-hand sword.
 Glou. True, uncle.
 Car. [*Aside to Gloucester*] Are ye advised?—the
  east side of the grove? 60
 Glou. [*Aside to Cardinal*] Cardinal, I am with you.
 King. Why, how now, uncle Gloucester!
 Glou. Talking of hawking; nothing else, my lord.
[*Aside to Cardinal*] Now, by God's Mother, priest,
  I'll shave your crown for this, 65
Or all my fence shall fail.
 Car. [*Aside to Gloucester*] *Medice, teipsum*—
Protector, see to't well, protect yourself.
 King. The winds grow high; so do your stomachs,
  lords. 70
How irksome is this music to my heart!
When such strings jar, what hope of harmony?
I pray, my lords, let me compound this strife.

   Enter [*a Townsman of St. Albans,*] *crying*
      "*A miracle!*"

 Glou. What means this noise?
Fellow, what miracle dost thou proclaim? 75
 Towns. A miracle! a miracle!

86. by his sight his sin be multiplied: i.e., he may yield to temptations that a blind man would be unaware of.

90. circumstance: details.

Suf. Come to the King and tell him what miracle.

Towns. Forsooth, a blind man at St. Alban's shrine,
Within this half-hour, hath received his sight;
A man that ne'er saw in his life before.   80

King. Now, God be praised, that to believing souls
Gives light in darkness, comfort in despair!

*Enter the Mayor of St. Albans and his brethren, bear-
ing Simpcox between two in a chair, [Simpcox's Wife
following].*

Car. Here comes the townsmen on procession
To present your Highness with the man.

King. Great is his comfort in this earthly vale,   85
Although by his sight his sin be multiplied.

Glou. Stand by, my masters: bring him near the
          King.
His Highness' pleasure is to talk with him.

King. Good fellow, tell us here the circumstance,   90
That we for thee may glorify the Lord.
What, hast thou been long blind and now restored?

Simp. Born blind, and't please your Grace.

Wife. Ay, indeed, was he.

Suf. What woman is this?   95

Wife. His wife, and't like your Worship.

Glou. Hadst thou been his mother, thou couldst
          have better told.

King. Where wert thou born?

Simp. At Berwick in the North, and't like your   100
          Grace.

104. unhallowed: unmarked by religious rites.
109. of: out of.

Suf. Come to the King and tell him what miracle.

Towns. Forsooth, a blind man at St. Alban's shrine,
Within this half-hour, hath received his sight;
A man that ne'er saw in his life before.   80

King. Now, God be praised, that to believing souls
Gives light in darkness, comfort in despair!

*Enter the Mayor of St. Albans and his brethren, bear-
ing Simpcox between two in a chair, [Simpcox's Wife
following].*

Car. Here comes the townsmen on procession
To present your Highness with the man.

King. Great is his comfort in this earthly vale,   85
Although by his sight his sin be multiplied.

Glou. Stand by, my masters: bring him near the
     King.
His Highness' pleasure is to talk with him.

King. Good fellow, tell us here the circumstance,   90
That we for thee may glorify the Lord.
What, hast thou been long blind and now restored?

Simp. Born blind, and't please your Grace.

Wife. Ay, indeed, was he.

Suf. What woman is this?   95

Wife. His wife, and't like your Worship.

Glou. Hadst thou been his mother, thou couldst
     have better told.

King. Where wert thou born?

Simp. At Berwick in the North, and't like your 100
     Grace.

104. unhallowed: unmarked by religious rites.
109. of: out of.

King. Poor soul, God's goodness hath been great to
   thee.
Let never day nor night unhallowed pass,
But still remember what the Lord hath done.   105
   Queen. Tell me good fellow, camest thou here by
   chance,
Or of devotion, to this holy shrine?
   Simp. God knows, of pure devotion; being called
A hundred times and oft'ner, in my sleep,   110
By good St. Alban, who said, "Simpcox, come,
Come, offer at my shrine, and I will help thee."
   Wife. Most true, forsooth; and many time and oft
Myself have heard a voice to call him so.
   Car. What, art thou lame?   115
   Simp.   Ay, God Almighty help me!
   Suf. How camest thou so?
   Simp.   A fall off of a tree.
   Wife. A plum tree, master.
   Glou.   How long hast thou been blind?   120
   Simp. Oh, born so, master.
   Glou.   What, and wouldst climb a tree?
   Simp. But that, in all my life, when I was a youth.
   Wife. Too true; and bought his climbing very dear.
   Glou. 'Mass, thou lovedst plums well, that wouldst   125
   venture so.
   Simp. Alas, good master, my wife desired some
   damsons
And made me climb, with danger of my life.
   Glou. A subtle knave! but yet it shall not serve.   130
Let me see thine eyes. Wink now. Now open them.
In my opinion yet thou seest not well.

157. nominate: name.

163. beadles: parish officials, one of whose duties was to beat rogues and other petty offenders.

Simp. Yes, master, clear as day, I thank God and
St. Alban.

Glou. Sayst thou me so? What color is this cloak of? 135

Simp. Red, master; red as blood.

Glou. Why, that's well said. What color is my gown
of?

Simp. Black, forsooth; coal black as jet.

King. Why, then, thou knowst what color jet is of? 140

Suf. And yet, I think, jet did he never see.

Glou. But cloaks and gowns, before this day, a
many.

Wife. Never, before this day, in all his life.

Glou. Tell me, sirrah, what's my name? 145

Simp. Alas, master, I know not.

Glou. What's his name?

Simp. I know not.

Glou. Nor his?

Simp. No, indeed, master. 150

Glou. What's thine own name?

Simp. Saunder Simpcox, and if it please you, master.

Glou. Then, Saunder, sit there, the lying'st knave
in Christendom. If thou hadst been born blind, thou
mightst as well have known all our names as thus to 155
name the several colors we do wear. Sight may distinguish of colors, but suddenly to nominate them all,
it is impossible. My lords, St. Alban here hath done a
miracle; and would ye not think his cunning to be
great that could restore this cripple to his legs again? 160

Simp. O master, that you could!

Glou. My masters of St. Albans, have you not
beadles in your town, and things called whips?

166. **straight:** immediately.
169. **leap me:** leap for me.
171. **go about:** undertake.
176. **doublet:** jacket.
181. **drab:** slattern; slut.

May. Yes, my lord, if it please your Grace.

Glou. Then send for one presently.   165

May. Sirrah, go fetch the beadle hither straight.

         Exit [an Attendant].

Glou. Now fetch me a stool hither by and by. Now, sirrah, if you mean to save yourself from whipping, leap me over this stool and run away.

Simp. Alas, master, I am not able to stand alone. 170 You go about to torture me in vain.

     Enter a Beadle with whips.

Glou. Well, sir, we must have you find your legs. Sirrah beadle, whip him till he leap over that same stool.

Bead. I will, my lord. Come on, sirrah: off with 175 your doublet quickly.

Simp. Alas, master, what shall I do? I am not able to stand.

After the Beadle hath hit him once, he leaps over the
  stool and runs away; and they follow and cry, "A
           miracle!"

King. O God, seest Thou this and bearest so long?

Queen. It made me laugh to see the villain run. 180

Glou. Follow the knave; and take this drab away.

Wife. Alas, sir, we did it for pure need.

Glou. Let them be whipped through every market town till they come to Berwick, from whence they came.   *Exeunt [Wife, Beadle, Mayor, etc.]* 185

Car. Duke Humphrey has done a miracle today.

192. **sort:** crew; **naughty:** wicked; **lewdly bent:** inclined to wickedness.

193–94. **Under the countenance and confederacy/Of:** sponsored and assisted by.

195. **rout:** company; gang.

196. **practiced:** plotted.

198. **fact:** act of wrongdoing.

200. **Demanding of:** asking questions about.

202. **at large:** fully.

205. **forthcoming:** in safe custody.

207. **like:** likely; **hour:** appointment (to fight).

208. **leave:** cease.

214. **confusion:** destruction.

Suf. True, made the lame to leap and fly away.
   Glou. But you have done more miracles than I;
You made in a day, my lord, whole towns to fly.

Enter Buckingham.

   King. What tidings with our cousin Buckingham?   190
   Buck. Such as my heart doth tremble to unfold.
A sort of naughty persons, lewdly bent,
Under the countenance and confederacy
Of Lady Eleanor, the Protector's wife,
The ringleader and head of all this rout,   195
Have practiced dangerously against your state,
Dealing with witches and with conjurers:
Whom we have apprehended in the fact;
Raising up wicked spirits from underground,
Demanding of King Henry's life and death,   200
And other of your Highness' Privy Council,
As more at large your Grace shall understand.
   Car. [*Aside to Gloucester*] And so, my Lord Pro-
      tector, by this means
Your lady is forthcoming yet at London.   205
This news, I think, hath turned your weapon's edge.
'Tis like, my lord, you will not keep your hour.
   Glou. Ambitious churchman, leave to afflict my
      heart:
Sorrow and grief have vanquished all my powers;   210
And, vanquished as I am, I yield to thee,
Or to the meanest groom.
   King. O God, what mischiefs work the wicked ones,
Heaping confusion on their own heads thereby!

215. **tainture:** stain; disgrace.

216. **thou wert best:** you had better.

222. **conversed:** consorted.

231. **poise:** balance; weigh.

232. **beam:** horizontal bar from which the balances are suspended.

[II.ii.] After supper, York asks Salisbury and Warwick to confirm or deny his title to the crown of England, which he traces from Edward III's third son, Lionel Duke of Clarence, while King Henry's claim derives from John of Gaunt, Edward's fourth son. Convinced, both nobles kneel and hail York as their sovereign. York thanks them but points out that he is not yet King and that they must wait until the other factious lords have ruined Gloucester. He prophesies that these same lords will also fall. Warwick declares that he will one day make York King of England; York in turn promises that he will make Warwick the greatest man in England next to the King.

4. **close:** private; hence, suitable for confidential talk.

Queen. Gloucester, see here the tainture of thy nest, 215
And look thyself be faultless, thou wert best.
　Glou. Madam, for myself, to Heaven I do appeal
How I have loved my king and commonweal.
And, for my wife, I know not how it stands:
Sorry I am to hear what I have heard. 220
Noble she is, but if she have forgot
Honor and virtue and conversed with such
As, like to pitch, defile nobility,
I banish her my bed and company
And give her as a prey to law and shame, 225
That hath dishonored Gloucester's honest name.
　King. Well, for this night we will repose us here.
Tomorrow toward London back again,
To look into this business thoroughly,
And call these foul offenders to their answers, 230
And poise the cause in Justice' equal scales,
Whose beam stands sure, whose rightful cause pre-
　　vails.

　　　　　　　　　　Flourish. Exeunt.

[Scene II. London. The Duke of York's garden.]

Enter York, Salisbury, and Warwick.

York. Now, my good lords of Salisbury and War-
　wick,
Our simple supper ended, give me leave
In this close walk to satisfy myself

5. **craving:** requesting.
6. **infallible:** certain; undeniable.
21. **Richard:** Richard II.
28. **Pomfret:** now known as Pontefract (Yorkshire).

Henry IV. From John Speed, *The Theatre of the Empire of Great Britain* (1627).

In craving your opinion of my title,　　　　　　　　　　5
Which is infallible, to England's crown.
　Sal. My lord, I long to hear it at full.
　War. Sweet York, begin: and if thy claim be good,
The Nevilles are thy subjects to command.
　York. Then thus:　　　　　　　　　　　　　　　10
Edward the Third, my lords, had seven sons:
The first, Edward the Black Prince, Prince of Wales;
The second, William of Hatfield, and the third,
Lionel Duke of Clarence; next to whom
Was John of Gaunt, the Duke of Lancaster;　　　　　15
The fifth was Edmund Langley, Duke of York;
The sixth was Thomas of Woodstock, Duke of Glou-
　　cester;
William of Windsor was the seventh and last.
Edward the Black Prince died before his father　　　20
And left behind him Richard, his only son,
Who after Edward the Third's death reigned as King;
Till Henry Bolingbroke, Duke of Lancaster,
The eldest son and heir of John of Gaunt,
Crowned by the name of Henry the Fourth,　　　　　25
Seized on the realm, deposed the rightful King,
Sent his poor queen to France, from whence she came,
And him to Pomfret, where, as all you know,
Harmless Richard was murdered traitorously.
　War. Father, the Duke hath told the truth:　　　30
Thus got the house of Lancaster the crown.
　York. Which now they hold by force and not by
　　right;
For Richard, the first son's heir, being dead,
The issue of the next son should have reigned.　　　35

43. This Edmund: Shakespeare follows the chroniclers in confusing Edmund, 5th Earl of March, with his uncle, the brother of Roger, 4th Earl of March. Henry IV's refusal to ransom Edmund was one of the grievances that caused the Percies to rebel in *1 Henry IV*.

62. issue fails: offspring die out.

Sal. But William of Hatfield died without an heir.

York. The third son, Duke of Clarence, from whose line
I claim the crown, had issue, Philippa, a daughter,
Who married Edmund Mortimer, Earl of March.   40
Edmund had issue, Roger Earl of March;
Roger had issue, Edmund, Anne, and Eleanor.

Sal. This Edmund, in the reign of Bolingbroke,
As I have read, laid claim unto the crown
And but for Owen Glendower had been King,   45
Who kept him in captivity till he died.
But to the rest.

York.   His eldest sister, Anne,
My mother, being heir unto the crown,
Married Richard Earl of Cambridge, who was son   50
To Edmund Langley, Edward the Third's fifth son.
By her I claim the kingdom: she was heir
To Roger Earl of March, who was the son
Of Edmund Mortimer, who married Philippa,
Sole daughter unto Lionel Duke of Clarence.   55
So, if the issue of the elder son
Succeed before the younger, I am King.

War. What plain proceedings is more plain than this?
Henry doth claim the crown from John of Gaunt,   60
The fourth son; York claims it from the third.
Till Lionel's issue fails, his should not reign.
It fails not yet but flourishes in thee
And in thy sons, fair slips of such a stock.
Then, father Salisbury, kneel we together;   65
And in this private plot be we the first

75. **advice:** discretion.
77. **Wink at:** overlook; ignore.

That shall salute our rightful sovereign
With honor of his birthright to the crown.
   Both. Long live our sovereign Richard, England's
    king!   70
   York. We thank you, lords. But I am not your king
Till I be crowned and that my sword be stained
With heartblood of the house of Lancaster;
And that's not suddenly to be performed,
But with advice and silent secrecy.   75
Do you as I do in these dangerous days:
Wink at the Duke of Suffolk's insolence,
At Beaufort's pride, at Somerset's ambition,
At Buckingham and all the crew of them,
Till they have snared the shepherd of the flock,   80
That virtuous prince, the good Duke Humphrey.
'Tis that they seek, and they in seeking that
Shall find their deaths, if York can prophesy.
   Sal. My lord, break we off: we know your mind at
    full.   85
   War. My heart assures me that the Earl of Warwick
Shall one day make the Duke of York a king.
   York. And, Neville, this I do assure myself:
Richard shall live to make the Earl of Warwick
The greatest man in England but the King.   90
                              Exeunt.

[II.iii.] The Duchess of Gloucester and her fellow culprits receive their sentences from the King: the witch is to be burned; the two priests are to be hanged; and the Duchess is to do three days' public penance and then to be imprisoned for life on the Isle of Man. Gloucester, deeply grieved, requests permission to retire; before he goes, the King asks for his staff of office and asserts that he will be his own Protector. The combat between Horner, the armorer, and his man, Peter, is ordered. Both men have been drinking heavily with their friends. Peter, who fears his master's superior skill in fighting, is certain that he will be killed but manages to give Horner a fatal blow. The latter confesses his treason before he dies.

▬▬▬▬▬▬▬▬▬▬▬▬

10. for: because.
21. age: old age.

[Scene III. A hall of justice.]

Sound trumpets. Enter the King, [the Queen, Glou-
cester, York, Suffolk, and Salisbury; the Duchess of
Gloucester, Margery Jourdain, Southwell, Hume, and
Bolingbroke, under guard].

   King. Stand forth, Dame Eleanor Cobham, Glou-
    cester's wife:
In sight of God and us your guilt is great:
Receive the sentence of the law for sins
Such as by God's book are adjudged to death.   5
You four, from hence to prison back again;
From thence unto the place of execution.
The witch in Smithfield shall be burned to ashes,
And you three shall be strangled on the gallows.
You, madam, for you are more nobly born,   10
Despoiled of your honor in your life,
Shall, after three days' open penance done,
Live in your country here in banishment,
With Sir John Stanley, in the Isle of Man.
   Duch. Welcome is banishment; welcome were my 15
    death.
   Glou. Eleanor, the law, thou seest, hath judged
    thee:
I cannot justify whom the law condemns.
         [Exeunt Duchess and other prisoners, guarded.]
Mine eyes are full of tears, my heart of grief.   20
Ah, Humphrey, this dishonor in thine age

24. **would:** craves; **mine age would ease:** my advanced years need rest.

32. **years:** maturity.

33. **be to be protected:** be in a position where protection is considered necessary.

35. **the King his realm:** the realm of the King (the old form of the possessive). A repetition of "give up" is understood.

46. **bears so shrewd a maim:** has received such a crippling blow; **pulls:** losses.

47. **limb:** support (his staff of office).

48. **raught:** attained; the old past tense of "reached."

50. **lofty pine:** great man; the pine was a common symbol of lofty birth or position; **hangs:** droops.

Will bring thy head with sorrow to the ground!
I beseech your Majesty, give me leave to go:
Sorrow would solace and mine age would ease.

   King. Stay, Humphrey Duke of Gloucester: ere 25
    thou go,
Give up thy staff. Henry will to himself
Protector be; and God shall be my hope,
My stay, my guide, and lantern to my feet.
And go in peace, Humphrey, no less beloved 30
Than when thou wert Protector to thy king.

   Queen. I see no reason why a king of years
Should be to be protected like a child.
God and King Henry govern England's realm.
Give up your staff, sir, and the King his realm. 35

   Glou. My staff? Here, noble Henry, is my staff.
As willingly do I the same resign
As e'er thy father Henry made it mine;
And even as willingly at thy feet I leave it
As others would ambitiously receive it. 40
Farewell, good King: when I am dead and gone,
May honorable peace attend thy throne!   *Exit.*

   Queen. Why, now is Henry king and Margaret
    queen
And Humphrey Duke of Gloucester scarce himself, 45
That bears so shrewd a maim: two pulls at once:
His lady banished, and a limb lopped off.
This staff of honor raught, there let it stand,
Where it best fits to be, in Henry's hand.

   Suf. Thus droops this lofty pine and hangs his 50
    sprays;
Thus Eleanor's pride dies in her youngest days.

53. **let him go:** forget him.

55. **appellant:** accuser.

56. **man:** apprentice.

60. **fit:** suitably arranged.

62. **worse bested:** worse placed; more daunted.

66. **sack:** sweet sherry.

68–9. **charneco:** a wine, possibly deriving its name from a Portuguese village of the same name.

70. **double:** i.e., strong.

72. **Let it come:** bring on the beer; pass it around.

73. **fig:** a term of contempt, often accompanied by an obscene gesture.

York. Lords, let him go. Please it your Majesty,
This is the day appointed for the combat;
And ready are the appellant and defendant,   55
The armorer and his man, to enter the lists,
So please your Highness to behold the fight.

Queen. Ay, good my lord; for purposely therefor
Left I the court, to see this quarrel tried.

King. O' God's name, see the lists and all things fit.   60
Here let them end it; and God defend the right!

York. I never saw a fellow worse bested,
Or more afraid to fight, than is the appellant,
The servant of this armorer, my lords.

*Enter at one door [Horner,] the Armorer, and his
Neighbors, drinking to him so much that he is drunk;
and he enters with a drum before him and his staff
with a sandbag fastened to it; and at the other door
[Peter,] his man, with a drum and sandbag, and
'Prentices drinking to him.*

1. Neigh. Here, neighbor Horner, I drink to you in   65
a cup of sack: and fear not, neighbor, you shall do
well enough.

2. Neigh. And here, neighbor, here's a cup of charneco.

3. Neigh. And here's a pot of good double beer,   70
neighbor: drink, and fear not your man.

Horn. Let it come, i' faith, and I'll pledge you all;
and a fig for Peter!

1. 'Pren. Here, Peter, I drink to thee: and be not
afraid.   75

80. **and if:** if.

94. **I will take my death:** I will stake my life on the matter.

95–6. **have at thee:** be warned; I shall attack thee.

97. **Dispatch:** hurry up.

2. 'Pren. Be merry, Peter, and fear not thy master:
fight for credit of the 'prentices.

Peter. I thank you all. Drink, and pray for me, I
pray you; for I think I have taken my last draught in
this world. Here, Robin, and if I die, I give thee my   80
apron; and, Will, thou shalt have my hammer; and
here, Tom, take all the money that I have. O Lord
bless me! I pray God! for I am never able to deal with
my master, he hath learnt so much fence already.

Sal. Come, leave your drinking and fall to blows.   85
Sirrah, what's thy name?

Peter. Peter, forsooth.

Sal. Peter! What more?

Peter. Thump.

Sal. Thump! then see thou thump thy master well.   90

Horn. Masters, I am come hither, as it were, upon
my man's instigation, to prove him a knave and myself an honest man. And, touching the Duke of York,
I will take my death, I never meant him any ill, nor
the King, nor the Queen: and therefore, Peter, have   95
at thee with a downright blow!

York. Dispatch: this knave's tongue begins to double. Sound, trumpets, alarum to the combatants!

[*Alarum.*] *They fight, and Peter strikes him down.*

Horn. Hold, Peter, hold! I confess, I confess treason.
[*Dies.*]

York. Take away his weapon. Fellow, thank God   100
and the good wine in thy master's way.

Peter. O God, have I overcome mine enemies in
this presence? O Peter, thou hast prevailed in right!

King. Go, take hence that traitor from our sight;

[II.iv.] Gloucester and servants witness the Duchess' public penance in the streets of London. The Duchess bewails her disgrace and reproaches her husband for condoning it. Gloucester can only counsel patience. Conscious of his own innocence, he brushes aside her warning that his failure to use the power at his disposal will lead to his own downfall. A herald summons Gloucester to a Parliament at Bury St. Edmunds and he bids goodby to his wife, who is to be escorted to the Isle of Man to fulfill the rest of her sentence.

▓▓▓▓▓▓▓▓▓▓▓▓▓▓▓▓▓▓▓▓▓▓

Ent. mourning cloaks: long cloaks with hoods, traditionally worn at funerals.
10. **Uneath:** with difficulty.
12. **abrook:** endure.
13. **abject:** mean; despicable.
14. **envious:** malicious.
15. **erst:** formerly.

For by his death we do perceive his guilt.   105
And God in justice hath revealed to us
The truth and innocence of this poor fellow,
Which he had thought to have murdered wrongfully.
Come, fellow, follow us for thy reward.

Sound a flourish. Exeunt.

[Scene IV. London. A street.]

Enter Gloucester and his Men, in mourning cloaks.

  Glou. Thus sometimes hath the brightest day a
    cloud;
And after summer evermore succeeds
Barren winter, with his wrathful, nipping cold:
So cares and joys abound, as seasons fleet.   5
Sirs, what's o'clock?
  Serv.   Ten, my lord.
  Glou. Ten is the hour that was appointed me
To watch the coming of my punished duchess:
Uneath may she endure the flinty streets,   10
To tread them with her tender-feeling feet.
Sweet Nell, ill can thy noble mind abrook
The abject people gazing on thy face,
With envious looks laughing at thy shame,
That erst did follow thy proud chariot wheels   15
When thou didst ride in triumph through the streets.
But, soft! I think she comes; and I'll prepare
My tear-stained eyes to see her miseries.

27. **closet:** chamber; **pent up:** confined.

28. **ban:** curse.

34. **Mailed:** wrapped in cloth (referring to the sheet she wears); a term from falconry; **papers:** a placard describing her crime.

36. **deep-fet:** brought forth from deep within herself; heartfelt. "Fet" is an old form of "fetched."

38. **start:** flinch in pain.

39. **advised:** careful.

41. **Trowest thou:** dost thou think.

Enter the Duchess in a white sheet, and a taper burn-
ing in her hand; with [Sir John Stanley,] the Sheriff,
and Officers.

Serv. So please your Grace, we'll take her from the
    sheriff.   20
Glou. No, stir not, for your lives: let her pass by.
Duch. Come you, my lord, to see my open shame?
Now thou dost penance too. Look how they gaze!
See how the giddy multitude do point,
And nod their heads, and throw their eyes on thee!   25
Ah, Gloucester, hide thee from their hateful looks,
And, in thy closet pent up, rue my shame
And ban thine enemies, both mine and thine!
Glou. Be patient, gentle Nell: forget this grief.
Duch. Ah, Gloucester, teach me to forget myself!   30
For whilst I think I am thy married wife,
And thou a prince, Protector of this land,
Methinks I should not thus be led along,
Mailed up in shame, with papers on my back,
And followed with a rabble that rejoice   35
To see my tears and hear my deep-fet groans.
The ruthless flint doth cut my tender feet,
And, when I start, the envious people laugh
And bid me be advised how I tread.
Ah, Humphrey, can I bear this shameful yoke?   40
Trowest thou that e'er I'll look upon the world
Or count them happy that enjoys the sun?
No: dark shall be my light and night my day.
To think upon my pomp shall be my hell.

45. **Sometime:** at one time.

48. **As:** that.

57. **limed bushes:** smeared bushes with birdlime; see I.[iii.]87.

61. **aimest all awry:** are quite mistaken.

62. **attainted:** convicted.

65. **scathe:** harm.

68. **scandal:** disgrace.

71. **sort:** dispose; order.

72. **These fews days' wonder will be quickly worn:** proverbially, "A wonder lasts but nine days"; i.e., this sensation will soon be forgotten.

Sometime I'll say, I am Duke Humphrey's wife,   45
And he a prince and ruler of the land:
Yet so he ruled, and such a prince he was,
As he stood by whilst I, his forlorn duchess,
Was made a wonder and a pointing-stock
To every idle rascal follower.   50
But be thou mild and blush not at my shame,
Nor stir at nothing till the ax of death
Hang over thee, as, sure, it shortly will;
For Suffolk—he that can do all in all
With her that hateth thee and hates us all—   55
And York, and impious Beaufort, that false priest,
Have all limed bushes to betray thy wings,
And, fly thou how thou canst, they'll tangle thee:
But fear not thou until thy foot be snared,
Nor never seek prevention of thy foes.   60

   Glou. Ah, Nell, forbear! Thou aimest all awry:
I must offend before I be attainted;
And, had I twenty times so many foes,
And each of them had twenty times their power,
All these could not procure me any scathe,   65
So long as I am loyal, true, and crimeless.
Wouldst have me rescue thee from this reproach?
Why, yet thy scandal were not wiped away
But I in danger for the breach of law.
Thy greatest help is quiet, gentle Nell.   70
I pray thee, sort thy heart to patience:
These few days' wonder will be quickly worn.

75. **Bury:** Bury St. Edmunds.

77. **close:** secret.

81. **stays:** ceases.

85. **given in charge:** ordered.

87. **Entreat:** treat.

88. **the world may laugh again:** i.e., Fortune may smile again on Gloucester.

Enter a Herald.

Her. I summon your Grace to His Majesty's Parlia-
ment,
Holden at Bury the first of this next month.   75
  Glou. And my consent ne'er asked herein before!
This is close dealing. Well, I will be there.
                              [*Exit Herald.*]
My Nell, I take my leave: and, master sheriff,
Let not her penance exceed the King's commission.
  Sher. And 't please your Grace, here my commission   80
    stays,
And Sir John Stanley is appointed now
To take her with him to the Isle of Man.
  Glou. Must you, Sir John, protect my lady here?
  Stan. So am I given in charge, may 't please your   85
    Grace.
  Glou. Entreat her not the worse in that I pray
You use her well: the world may laugh again;
And I may live to do you kindness if
You do it her: and so, Sir John, farewell!   90
  Duch. What, gone, my lord, and bid me not fare-
    well!
  Glou. Witness my tears, I cannot stay to speak.
                  Exeunt Gloucester [*and Servingmen*].
  Duch. Art thou gone too? All comfort go with thee!
For none abides with me: my joy is death—   95
Death, at whose name I oft have been afeard,
Because I wished this world's eternity.
Stanley, I prithee, go and take me hence;

108. **conduct:** conductor.
109. **office:** duty.

I care not whither, for I beg no favor,
Only convey me where thou art commanded.   100
    Stan. Why, madam, that is to the Isle of Man,
There to be used according to your state.
    Duch. That's bad enough, for I am but reproach:
And shall I then be used reproachfully?
    Stan. Like to a duchess and Duke Humphrey's lady; 105
According to that state you shall be used.
    Duch. Sheriff, farewell, and better than I fare,
Although thou hast been conduct of my shame.
    Sher. It is my office, and, madam, pardon me.
    Duch. Ay, ay, farewell; thy office is discharged.   110
Come, Stanley, shall we go?
    Stan. Madam, your penance done, throw off this
        sheet,
And go we to attire you for our journey.
    Duch. My shame will not be shifted with my sheet: 115
No, it will hang upon my richest robes
And show itself, attire me how I can.
Go, lead the way: I long to see my prison.
                                        Exeunt.

THE SECOND PART
OF
HENRY THE SIXTH

ACT III

[III.i.] Gloucester is the last to arrive at the Parliament, which gives his enemies time to accuse him of complicity in the Duchess' conjurations and to warn the King that he is a menace. The King is convinced of Gloucester's loyalty and virtue. Nevertheless, when Gloucester arrives and Suffolk announces that he is under arrest, the King does not interfere but only expresses a hope that Gloucester will prove himself innocent. The King is so distressed at the arrest of his uncle that he refuses to sit in the Parliament and gives the nobles permission to make any decisions they wish without him. With the pious King absent, the nobles agree that Gloucester should be killed; Suffolk and the Cardinal undertake to see that it is done promptly. Word of rebellion in Ireland provokes a fresh quarrel between York and Somerset, but York is at length chosen to command forces to put down the rebels. Privately, York is pleased at having command of troops whom he can use for his own ends. He reveals that he has stirred to insurrection one Jack Cade. If Cade's rebellion is successful, York will come from Ireland with his men and take advantage of the turmoil to unseat King Henry and claim the throne.

▬▬▬▬▬▬▬▬▬▬

1. **muse:** wonder.
2. **wont:** habit.
9. **since:** when.
10. **glance a far-off look:** glance vaguely in his direction.
12. **admired:** wondered at.
17. **duty:** respect.

[ACT III]

[Scene I. The Abbey at Bury St. Edmunds.]

Sound a sennet. Enter King, Queen, Cardinal, Suffolk,
York, Buckingham, Salisbury, and Warwick to the
Parliament.

   King. I muse my lord of Gloucester is not come:
'Tis not his wont to be the hindmost man,
Whate'er occasion keeps him from us now.
   Queen. Can you not see? or will ye not observe
The strangeness of his altered countenance?   5
With what a majesty he bears himself,
How insolent of late he is become,
How proud, how peremptory, and unlike himself?
We know the time since he was mild and affable,
And if we did but glance a far-off look,   10
Immediately he was upon his knee,
That all the court admired him for submission:
But meet him now, and, be it in the morn,
When everyone will give the time of day,
He knits his brow and shows an angry eye   15
And passeth by with stiff unbowed knee,
Disdaining duty that to us belongs.

48

18. **grin:** bare their teeth.
19. **the lion:** symbolic of royalty.
23. **Meseemeth:** it seems to me; **policy:** wisdom.
24. **Respecting:** considering.
29. **make commotion:** stir up rebellion.
32. **Suffer:** allow.
33. **husbandry:** prudent management.
35. **collect:** notice.
36. **fond:** foolish.
38. **subscribe:** submit; yield.
40. **Reprove:** disprove.
41. **effectual:** conclusive.
45. **subornation:** prompting.
46. **practices:** plots.
47. **privy:** accessory.
48. **reputing of:** considering; making much of.

Small curs are not regarded when they grin;
But great men tremble when the lion roars;
And Humphrey is no little man in England.   20
First, note that he is near you in descent,
And, should you fall, he is the next will mount.
Meseemeth then it is no policy,
Respecting what a rancorous mind he bears,
And his advantage following your decease,   25
That he should come about your royal person
Or be admitted to your Highness' Council.
By flattery hath he won the commons' hearts,
And when he please to make commotion,
'Tis to be feared they all will follow him.   30
Now 'tis the spring, and weeds are shallow-rooted;
Suffer them now and they'll o'ergrow the garden
And choke the herbs for want of husbandry.
The reverent care I bear unto my lord
Made me collect these dangers in the Duke.   35
If it be fond, call it a woman's fear;
Which fear if better reasons can supplant,
I will subscribe and say I wronged the Duke.
My lord of Suffolk, Buckingham, and York,
Reprove my allegation, if you can;   40
Or else conclude my words effectual.

    Suf. Well hath your Highness seen into this duke;
And, had I first been put to speak my mind,
I think I should have told your Grace's tale.
The Duchess by his subornation,   45
Upon my life, began her devilish practices:
Or, if he were not privy to those faults,
Yet, by reputing of his high descent,

50. **vaunts:** boasts.

51. **bedlam brainsick:** lunatic (like an inmate of Bethlehem [Bedlam] Hospital, a London institution for the insane).

54. **simple show:** innocent appearance.

57. **Unsounded:** not plumbed to the depths; imperfectly revealed.

64. **to:** compared with: **faults unknown:** the faults not yet discovered.

67. **at once:** first of all.

68. **annoy:** wound.

69. **shall I speak my conscience:** if I say what I really think.

73. **well given:** well disposed; good.

74. **on:** of.

75–6. **fond affiance:** foolish faith.

As next the King he was successive heir,
And such high vaunts of his nobility,   50
Did instigate the bedlam brainsick Duchess
By wicked means to frame our sovereign's fall.
Smooth runs the water where the brook is deep;
And in his simple show he harbors treason.
The fox barks not when he would steal the lamb.   55
No, no, my sovereign; Gloucester is a man
Unsounded yet and full of deep deceit.

   Car. Did he not, contrary to form of law,
Devise strange deaths for small offenses done?

   York. And did he not, in his protectorship,   60
Levy great sums of money through the realm,
For soldiers' pay in France, and never sent it?
By means whereof the towns each day revolted.

   Buck. Tut, these are petty faults to faults unknown,
Which time will bring to light in smooth Duke   65
    Humphrey.

   King. My lords, at once: the care you have of us,
To mow down thorns that would annoy our foot,
Is worthy praise: but, shall I speak my conscience,
Our kinsman Gloucester is as innocent   70
From meaning treason to our royal person
As is the sucking lamb or harmless dove:
The Duke is virtuous, mild, and too well given
To dream on evil or to work my downfall.

   Queen. Ah, what's more dangerous than this fond   75
    affiance!
Seems he a dove? his feathers are but borrowed,
For he's disposed as the hateful raven.
Is he a lamb? his skin is surely lent him,

87. **interest:** legal right.
96. **gear:** matter.

For he's inclined as is the ravenous wolves.   80
Who cannot steal a shape that means deceit?
Take heed, my lord; the welfare of us all
Hangs on the cutting short that fraudful man.

Enter Somerset.

  Som. All health unto my gracious sovereign!
  King. Welcome, Lord Somerset. What news from   85
    France?
  Som. That all your interest in those territories
Is utterly bereft you: all is lost.
  King. Cold news, Lord Somerset: but God's will be
    done!   90
  York. [*Aside*] Cold news for me; for I had hope of
    France
As firmly as I hope for fertile England.
Thus are my blossoms blasted in the bud
And caterpillars eat my leaves away;   95
But I will remedy this gear ere long,
Or sell my title for a glorious grave.

Enter Gloucester.

  Glou. All happiness unto my lord the King!
Pardon, my Liege, that I have stayed so long.
  Suf. Nay, Gloucester, know that thou art come too   100
    soon,
Unless thou wert more loyal than thou art.
I do arrest thee of high treason here.
  Glou. Well, Suffolk, thou shalt not see me blush

108. **clear:** innocent.
118. **watched:** stayed awake.
119. **studying:** planning.
120. **doit:** small Dutch coin.
121. **groat:** coin valued at fourpence.
123. **proper:** personal.
125. **dispursed:** disbursed; spent.

Nor change my countenance for this arrest.　　　　　105
A heart unspotted is not easily daunted.
The purest spring is not so free from mud
As I am clear from treason to my sovereign.
Who can accuse me? Wherein am I guilty?
　　York. 'Tis thought, my lord, that you took bribes of　110
　　　　France,
And, being Protector, stayed the soldiers' pay;
By means whereof His Highness hath lost France.
　　Glou. Is it but thought so? What are they that
　　　　think it?　　　　　　　　　　　　　　　　115
I never robbed the soldiers of their pay,
Nor ever had one penny bribe from France.
So help me God, as I have watched the night,
Ay, night by night, in studying good for England!
That doit that e'er I wrested from the King,　　　120
Or any groat I hoarded to my use,
Be brought against me at my trial day!
No: many a pound of mine own proper store,
Because I would not tax the needy commons,
Have I dispursed to the garrisons,　　　　　　　125
And never asked for restitution.
　　Car. It serves you well, my lord, to say so much.
　　Glou. I say no more than truth, so help me God!
　　York. In your protectorship you did devise
Strange tortures for offenders never heard of,　　130
That England was defamed by tyranny.
　　Glou. Why, 'tis well known that, whiles I was Pro-
　　　　tector,
Pity was all the fault that was in me;
For I should melt at an offender's tears,　　　　135

136. **lowly:** humble.
138. **passengers:** travelers.
139. **condign:** deserved.
141. **what trespass else:** any other misdeed.
150. **suspense:** doubt.
156. **equity:** justice.
157. **complot:** conspiracy.
159. **period:** end.

And lowly words were ransom for their fault.
Unless it were a bloody murderer,
Or foul felonious thief that fleeced poor passengers,
I never gave them condign punishment:
Murder indeed, that bloody sin, I tortured   140
Above the felon or what trespass else.

Suf. My lord, these faults are easy, quickly answered:
But mightier crimes are laid unto your charge,
Whereof you cannot easily purge yourself.   145
I do arrest you in His Highness' name
And here commit you to my lord Cardinal
To keep, until your further time of trial.

King. My lord of Gloucester, 'tis my special hope
That you will clear yourself from all suspense: 150
My conscience tells me you are innocent.

Glou. Ah, gracious lord, these days are dangerous:
Virtue is choked with foul ambition
And charity chased hence by rancor's hand;
Foul subornation is predominant   155
And equity exiled your Highness' land.
I know their complot is to have my life;
And if my death might make this island happy,
And prove the period of their tyranny,
I would expend it with all willingness: 160
But mine is made the prologue to their play;
For thousands more, that yet suspect no peril,
Will not conclude their plotted tragedy.
Beaufort's red sparkling eyes blab his heart's malice
And Suffolk's cloudy brow his stormy hate;   165
Sharp Buckingham unburdens with his tongue

167. **envious:** hostile.

168. **dogged York, that reaches at the moon:** an allusion to the proverb "The moon does not heed the barking of dogs."

169. **overweening:** presumptuous.

170. **level:** aim.

174. **liefest:** dearest.

176. **conventicles:** meetings.

178. **want:** lack.

185. **rated:** scolded.

186. **scope of speech:** full freedom of speech.

188. **twit:** twitted; taunted.

189. **clerkly couched:** cleverly phrased.

192. **give the loser leave to chide:** allow the loser his say; proverbial.

194. **Beshrew:** curse.

196. **wrest:** distort.

Dog barking at the moon, emblem of presumptuous ambition. From Geoffrey Whitney, *A Choice of Emblems* (1586).

54

The envious load that lies upon his heart;
And dogged York, that reaches at the moon,
Whose overweening arm I have plucked back,
By false accuse doth level at my life:　　　　　　170
And you, my sovereign lady, with the rest,
Causeless have laid disgraces on my head,
And with your best endeavor have stirred up
My liefest liege to be mine enemy.
Ay, all of you have laid your heads together—　　175
Myself had notice of your conventicles—
And all to make away my guiltless life.
I shall not want false witness to condemn me,
Nor store of treasons to augment my guilt.
The ancient proverb will be well effected:　　　180
"A staff is quickly found to beat a dog."

　　Car. My Liege, his railing is intolerable:
If those that care to keep your royal person
From treason's secret knife and traitors' rage
Be thus upbraided, chid, and rated at,　　　　185
And the offender granted scope of speech,
'Twill make them cool in zeal unto your Grace.

　　Suf. Hath he not twit our sovereign lady here
With ignominious words, though clerkly couched,
As if she had suborned some to swear　　　　190
False allegations to o'erthrow his state?

　　Queen. But I can give the loser leave to chide.

　　Glou. Far truer spoke than meant. I lose, indeed:
Beshrew the winners, for they played me false!
And well such losers may have leave to speak.　195

　　Buck. He'll wrest the sense and hold us here all day:
Lord Cardinal, he is your prisoner.

202. **gnarling:** snarling.
218. **lowering star:** frowning planet; referring to the belief that heavenly bodies influenced men's fates.
220. **subversion:** overthrow; ruin.
227. **Looking:** seeking.

Car. Sirs, take away the Duke, and guard him sure.
Glou. Ah! thus King Henry throws away his crutch,
Before his legs be firm to bear his body.   200
Thus is the shepherd beaten from thy side,
And wolves are gnarling who shall gnaw thee first.
Ah, that my fear were false! ah, that it were!
For, good King Henry, thy decay I fear.
                                        Exit, [guarded].
    King. My lords, what to your wisdoms seemeth best, 205
Do or undo, as if ourself were here.
    Queen. What, will your Highness leave the Parliament?
    King. Ay, Margaret: my heart is drowned with grief,   210
Whose flood begins to flow within mine eyes,
My body round engirt with misery;
For what's more miserable than discontent?
Ah, uncle Humphrey! in thy face I see
The map of honor, truth, and loyalty: 215
And yet, good Humphrey, is the hour to come
That e'er I proved thee false or feared thy faith.
What lowering star now envies thy estate
That these great lords and Margaret our queen
Do seek subversion of thy harmless life?   220
Thou never didst them wrong nor no man wrong:
And as the butcher takes away the calf,
And binds the wretch, and beats it when it strays,
Bearing it to the bloody slaughterhouse,
Even so remorseless have they borne him hence;   225
And as the dam runs lowing up and down,
Looking the way her harmless young one went,

235. **Free:** generous.

237. **cold:** apathetic; passive.

239. **Beguiles:** deceives. The crocodile was reported by travelers to weep copiously and take his victims off guard.

242. **checkered:** variegated; **slough:** skin. The bestiaries described a speckled snake (perhaps the coral snake) that enchanted the onlooker with its beauty.

245. **wit:** wisdom.

249. **color:** pretext; excuse.

250. **meet:** suitable.

251. **were:** would be.

253. **haply:** perhaps.

"Cold snow melts with the sun's hot beams." From Geoffrey Whitney, *A Choice of Emblems* (1586).

And can do nought but wail her darling's loss,
Even so myself bewails good Gloucester's case
With sad unhelpful tears and with dimmed eyes   230
Look after him and cannot do him good,
So mighty are his vowed enemies.
His fortunes I will weep, and 'twixt each groan
Say "Who's a traitor? Gloucester he is none."
Exeunt [all but Queen, Cardinal Beaufort, Suffolk,
                and York. Somerset remains apart].
     Queen. Free lords, cold snow melts with the sun's   235
          hot beams.
Henry my lord is cold in great affairs,
Too full of foolish pity, and Gloucester's show
Beguiles him, as the mournful crocodile
With sorrow snares relenting passengers,   240
Or as the snake rolled in a flow'ring bank,
With shining checkered slough, doth sting a child
That for the beauty thinks it excellent.
Believe me, lords, were none more wise than I—
And yet herein I judge mine own wit good—   245
This Gloucester should be quickly rid the world,
To rid us from the fear we have of him.
     Car. That he should die is worthy policy;
But yet we want a color for his death:
'Tis meet he be condemned by course of law.   250
     Suf. But, in my mind, that were no policy:
The King will labor still to save his life,
The commons haply rise, to save his life;
And yet we have but trivial argument,
More than mistrust, that shows him worthy death.   255
     York. So that, by this, you would not have him die.

257. **fain:** willing; eager.

261. **Were't not all one:** would it not amount to the same thing as if.

268. **surveyor:** guardian.

270. **idly posted over:** carelessly dismissed.

274. **chaps:** jaws.

276. **stand on quillets:** hesitate over fine points.

277. **gins:** nets or traps.

280. **mates:** confounds.

287. **be his priest:** perform his last rites; see to his dispatch.

The result of leaving a fox to guard the sheep. From *Le microcosme* (n.d.).

Suf. Ah, York, no man alive so fain as I!

York. 'Tis York that hath more reason for his death.
But, my lord Cardinal, and you, my lord of Suffolk,
Say as you think, and speak it from your souls: 260
Were't not all one an empty eagle were set
To guard the chicken from a hungry kite,
As place Duke Humphrey for the King's Protector?

   Queen. So the poor chicken should be sure of
    death.   265

   Suf. Madam, 'tis true; and were 't not madness,
    then,
To make the fox surveyor of the fold?
Who being accused a crafty murderer,
His guilt should be but idly posted over,   270
Because his purpose is not executed.
No: let him die, in that he is a fox,
By nature proved an enemy to the flock,
Before his chaps be stained with crimson blood,
As Humphrey, proved by reasons, to my Liege.   275
And do not stand on quillets how to slay him:
Be it by gins, by snares, by subtlety,
Sleeping or waking, 'tis no matter how,
So he be dead; for that is good deceit
Which mates him first that first intends deceit.   280

   Queen. Thrice-noble Suffolk, 'tis resolutely spoke.

   Suf. Not resolute, except so much were done;
For things are often spoke and seldom meant:
But that my heart accordeth with my tongue,
Seeing the deed is meritorious,   285
And to preserve my sovereign from his foe,
Say but the word, and I will be his priest.

290. **censure:** judge.

292. **tender:** cherish.

296. **skills:** matters; **impugns our doom:** criticizes our sentence.

297. **amain:** with all speed.

300. **betime:** promptly.

302. **green:** fresh.

303. **breach:** gap; **expedient:** effectual; **stop:** filling-up.

308. **far-fet:** far-fetched; ingenious.

315. **charactered:** marked.

Car. But I would have him dead, my lord of Suffolk,
Ere you can take due orders for a priest.
Say you consent and censure well the deed,　　　　　290
And I'll provide his executioner,
I tender so the safety of my Liege.
　　Suf. Here is my hand, the deed is worthy doing.
　　Queen. And so say I.
　　York. And I: and now we three have spoke it,　　295
It skills not greatly who impugns our doom.

Enter a Post.

　　Post. Great lords, from Ireland am I come amain,
To signify that rebels there are up
And put the Englishmen unto the sword.
Send succors, lords, and stop the rage betime,　　　300
Before the wound do grow uncurable;
For, being green, there is great hope of help.
　　Car. A breach that craves a quick expedient stop!
What counsel give you in this weighty cause?
　　York. That Somerset be sent as regent thither.　　305
'Tis meet that lucky ruler be employed;
Witness the fortune he hath had in France.
　　Som. If York, with all his far-fet policy,
Had been the regent there instead of me,
He never would have stayed in France so long.　　310
　　York. No, not to lose it all, as thou hast done.
I rather would have lost my life betimes
Than bring a burden of dishonor home,
By staying there so long till all were lost.
Show me one scar charactered on thy skin:　　　315

317. **Nay, then:** enough of this bickering.
321. **happily:** haply; perhaps.
326. **kerns:** foot soldiers, but used loosely for a class of men who lived by spoil and pillage.
330. **hap:** luck.
331. **so please:** if it please.
336. **take order for:** arrange.
337. **charge:** responsibility.

Men's flesh preserved so whole do seldom win.

  Queen. Nay, then, this spark will prove a raging fire,
If wind and fuel be brought to feed it with.
No more, good York; sweet Somerset, be still.
Thy fortune, York, hadst thou been regent there,   320
Might happily have proved far worse than his.

  York. What, worse than nought? Nay, then, a shame
    take all!

  Som. And, in the number, thee that wishest shame!

  Car. My lord of York, try what your fortune is.   325
The uncivil kerns of Ireland are in arms
And temper clay with blood of Englishmen.
To Ireland will you lead a band of men,
Collected choicely, from each county some,
And try your hap against the Irishmen?   330

  York. I will, my lord, so please His Majesty.

  Suf. Why, our authority is his consent,
And what we do establish he confirms.
Then, noble York, take thou this task in hand.

  York. I am content: provide me soldiers, lords,   335
Whiles I take order for mine own affairs.

  Suf. A charge, Lord York, that I will see performed.
But now return we to the false Duke Humphrey.

  Car. No more of him; for I will deal with him,
That henceforth he shall trouble us no more.   340
And so break off: the day is almost spent.
Lord Suffolk, you and I must talk of that event.

  York. My lord of Suffolk, within fourteen days
At Bristol I expect my soldiers;
For there I'll ship them all for Ireland.   345

348. **misdoubt:** indecision.

351. **keep:** stay.

355. **dignity:** high estate (specifically, sovereignty).

360. **starved snake:** referring to the fable of the chilled snake that was warmed by the countryman, who was stung to death when the snake revived.

368. **fell:** deadly.

369. **circuit:** circle; crown.

370. **transparent:** penetrating; pervasive.

371. **mad-bred flaw:** outburst of madness.

372. **minister:** agent.

Suf. I'll see it truly done, my lord of York.

　　　　　　　　　　　　Exeunt [all but York].

York. Now, York, or never, steel thy fearful thoughts
And change misdoubt to resolution.
Be that thou hopest to be, or what thou art
Resign to death; it is not worth the enjoying.　　　　　350
Let pale-faced fear keep with the mean-born man,
And find no harbor in a royal heart.
Faster than springtime show'rs comes thought on
　　　thought,
And not a thought but thinks on dignity.　　　　　355
My brain, more busy than the laboring spider,
Weaves tedious snares to trap mine enemies.
Well, nobles, well, 'tis politicly done
To send me packing with an host of men!
I fear me you but warm the starved snake,　　　　　360
Who, cherished in your breasts, will sting your hearts.
'Twas men I lacked, and you will give them me.
I take it kindly; yet, be well assured,
You put sharp weapons in a madman's hands.
Whiles I in Ireland nourish a mighty band,　　　　　365
I will stir up in England some black storm
Shall blow ten thousand souls to Heaven or hell;
And this fell tempest shall not cease to rage
Until the golden circuit on my head,
Like to the glorious sun's transparent beams,　　　　　370
Do calm the fury of this mad-bred flaw.
And, for a minister of my intent,
I have seduced a headstrong Kentishman,
John Cade of Ashford,
To make commotion, as full well he can,　　　　　375

379. **darts:** the usual weapon of the lightly-armed kern.

380. **porpentine:** porcupine.

382. **Morisco:** morris dancer.

383. **bells:** the costume of the morris dancer was usually trimmed with bells.

384. **shag-haired:** having hair crudely chopped.

385. **conversed:** consorted.

389. **For that:** because; **John Mortimer:** a fictitious character; there was no John in the Mortimer family, and Cade's whole story was a politic fiction.

392. **affect:** incline to.

396. **great like:** very likely.

400. **put apart:** set aside; dethroned.

Porpentine, with quills erect. From Henry Topsell, *History of Four-Footed Beasts* (1658).

Under the title of John Mortimer.
In Ireland have I seen this stubborn Cade
Oppose himself against a troop of kerns,
And fought so long till that his thighs with darts
Were almost like a sharp-quilled porpentine;   380
And, in the end being rescued, I have seen
Him caper upright like a wild Morisco,
Shaking the bloody darts as he his bells.
Full often, like a shag-haired crafty kern,
Hath he conversed with the enemy   385
And undiscovered come to me again
And given me notice of their villainies.
This devil here shall be my substitute;
For that John Mortimer, which now is dead,
In face, in gait, in speech, he doth resemble.   390
By this I shall perceive the commons' mind,
How they affect the house and claim of York.
Say he be taken, racked, and tortured,
I know no pain they can inflict upon him
Will make him say I moved him to those arms.   395
Say that he thrive, as 'tis great like he will,
Why, then from Ireland come I with my strength
And reap the harvest which that rascal sowed;
For Humphrey being dead, as he shall be,
And Henry put apart, the next for me.   400

Exit.

[III.ii.] The murder of Gloucester is reported to Suffolk by the assassins he hired. When the King, the Queen, and other nobles appear, the King orders Gloucester summoned; Suffolk returns with word of his death. The King faints and when revived laments Gloucester's death and berates Suffolk for being his enemy. The Queen attempts to distract his attention by pretending to be aggrieved at her husband's uncontrolled grief over Gloucester. Warwick and Salisbury report that the people have already heard the news and blame the Cardinal and Suffolk. Gloucester's corpse is brought into the King's presence, and Warwick points out signs on the face that suggest a violent death. He accuses Suffolk and the Cardinal. The people are threatening a disturbance outside; Salisbury reports that unless Suffolk is executed or banished, the mob intends to drag him from the King's protection and torture him to death. The King needs little convincing and readily exiles Suffolk on pain of death. Alone, the Queen and Suffolk alternate passionate and sorrowful farewells with curses on their enemies. News that the Cardinal is at the point of death has little effect now. At length, fearing the King's return, Suffolk and the Queen go their separate ways.

<hr/>

3. **to do:** i.e., not done.
8. **well said:** well done.
15. **straight:** immediately.
17. **published:** declared.

[Scene II. Bury St. Edmunds. A room of state.]

Enter two or three [Murderers] running over the
stage, from the murder of Duke Humphrey.

1. Mur. Run to my lord of Suffolk; let him know
We have dispatched the Duke, as he commanded.
2. Mur. Oh that it were to do! What have we done?
Didst ever hear a man so penitent?

Enter Suffolk.

1. Mur. Here comes my lord.   5
Suf. Now, sirs, have you dispatched this thing?
1. Mur. Ay, my good lord, he's dead.
Suf. Why, that's well said. Go, get you to my house:
I will reward you for this venturous deed.
The King and all the peers are here at hand.   10
Have you laid fair the bed? Is all things well,
According as I gave directions?
1. Mur. 'Tis, my good lord.
Suf. Awayl be gone.   *Exeunt [Murderers].*

Sound trumpets. Enter the King, the Queen, Cardinal,
Somerset, with Attendants.

King. Go, call our uncle to our presence straight;   15
Say we intend to try His Grace today,
If he be guilty, as 'tis published.

18. **presently:** at once.
20. **straiter:** more severely.
22. **approved:** proved.
25. **him:** himself.
31. **forfend:** forbid.
36. **wring him by the nose:** a method of improving circulation.
44. **a raven's note:** the croak of a raven was proverbially an ominous sound.

Suf. I'll call him presently, my noble lord.   *Exit.*

King. Lords, take your places; and, I pray you all,

Proceed no straiter 'gainst our uncle Gloucester   20

Than from true evidence of good esteem

He be approved in practice culpable.

Queen. God forbid any malice should prevail

That faultless may condemn a nobleman!

Pray God he may acquit him of suspicion!   25

King. I thank thee, Meg; these words content me
     much.

Enter Suffolk.

How now! why lookst thou pale? Why tremblest thou?

Where is our uncle? What's the matter, Suffolk?

Suf. Dead in his bed, my lord: Gloucester is dead.   30

Queen. Marry, God forfend!

Car. God's secret judgment! I did dream tonight

The Duke was dumb and could not speak a word.

                         [The] King swoons.

Queen. How fares my lord? Help, lords! the King is
     dead.   35

Som. Rear up his body; wring him by the nose.

Queen. Run, go, help, help! O Henry, ope thine eyes!

Suf. He doth revive again: madam, be patient.

King. O heavenly God!

Queen.   How fares my gracious lord?   40

Suf. Comfort, my sovereign! gracious Henry, com-
     fort!

King. What, doth my lord of Suffolk comfort me?

Came he right now to sing a raven's note,

47. **from a hollow breast:** insincerely.

56. **basilisk:** a fabulous reptile reputed to kill with its glance.

60. **rate:** scold.

64. **heart-offending:** groans were supposed to weaken the heart.

65. **blood-consuming:** sighs were believed to use up blood.

67. **pale as primrose:** the primrose, because of its color, was associated with anemia.

69. **deem:** judge.

70. **hollow:** insincere, as in line 47.

Whose dismal tune bereft my vital pow'rs,   45
And thinks he that the chirping of a wren,
By crying comfort from a hollow breast,
Can chase away the first conceived sound?
Hide not thy poison with such sugared words;
Lay not thy hands on me. Forbear, I say;   50
Their touch affrights me as a serpent's sting.
Thou baleful messenger, out of my sight!
Upon thy eyeballs murderous tyranny
Sits in grim majesty, to fright the world.
Look not upon me, for thine eyes are wounding.   55
Yet do not go away: come, basilisk,
And kill the innocent gazer with thy sight;
For in the shade of death I shall find joy,
In life but double death, now Gloucester's dead.
    Queen. Why do you rate my lord of Suffolk thus?   60
Although the Duke was enemy to him,
Yet he most Christian-like laments his death.
And for myself, foe as he was to me,
Might liquid tears, or heart-offending groans,
Or blood-consuming sighs recall his life,   65
I would be blind with weeping, sick with groans,
Look pale as primrose with blood-drinking sighs,
And all to have the noble Duke alive.
What know I how the world may deem of me?
For it is known we were but hollow friends.   70
It may be judged I made the Duke away;
So shall my name with slander's tongue be wounded
And princes' courts be filled with my reproach.
This get I by his death. Ay me, unhappy!
To be a queen and crowned with infamy!   75

76. woe is me: woeful am I.

80. adder: the asp was believed to stop its ear against the snake-charmer's music; see also Psalm 58:4-5; **waxen:** grown.

87. awkward: blowing the wrong way; contrary.

93. he: Aeolus, god of the winds, who kept them secured in a cave.

98. pretty vaulting: gently lapping, instead of rolling in rough billows.

104. Because: in order that.

106. ken: spy; sight.

King. Ah, woe is me for Gloucester, wretched man!
  Queen. Be woe for me, more wretched than he is.
What, dost thou turn away and hide thy face?
I am no loathsome leper: look on me.
What! art thou, like the adder, waxen deaf?   80
Be poisonous too and kill thy forlorn queen.
Is all thy comfort shut in Gloucester's tomb?
Why, then, Dame Margaret was ne'er thy joy.
Erect his statue and worship it,
And make my image but an alehouse sign.   85
Was I for this nigh wracked upon the sea,
And twice by awkward wind from England's bank
Drove back again unto my native clime?
What boded this but well-forewarning wind
Did seem to say, "Seek not a scorpion's nest,   90
Nor set no footing on this unkind shore"?
What did I then but cursed the gentle gusts
And he that loosed them forth their brazen caves,
And bid them blow toward England's blessed shore,
Or turn our stern upon a dreadful rock?   95
Yet Aeolus would not be a murderer
But left that hateful office unto thee:
The pretty vaulting sea refused to drown me,
Knowing that thou wouldst have me drowned on
     shore   100
With tears as salt as sea, through thy unkindness.
The splitting rocks cow'red in the sinking sands
And would not dash me with their ragged sides,
Because thy flinty heart, more hard then they,
Might in thy palace perish Margaret.   105
As far as I could ken thy chalky cliffs,

116. **be packing with my heart:** i.e., follow the diamond heart so as to regain sight of England.

117. **spectacles:** organs of sight.

120. **agent of . . . inconstancy:** proxy for the marriage and thus responsible also for Henry's inconstancy.

121. **witch:** bewitch; **Ascanius:** son of Aeneas. Venus sent Cupid disguised as Ascanius to inspire Dido, Queen of Carthage, with love of Aeneas, in order to assure him of her help (Vergil, *Aeneid*, bk. i).

122. **madding:** becoming mad with love.

130. **The commons, like an angry hive of bees:** the comparison of the state with a beehive was an Elizabethan commonplace.

131. **want:** lack.

133. **spleenful:** angry.

Dido and Aeneas. From Guillaume Rouillé, *Promptuarii iconum* (1553).

When from thy shore the tempest beat us back,
I stood upon the hatches in the storm;
And when the dusky sky began to rob
My earnest-gaping sight of thy land's view,   110
I took a costly jewel from my neck—
A heart it was, bound in with diamonds—
And threw it toward thy land. The sea received it,
And so I wished thy body might my heart;
And even with this I lost fair England's view   115
And bid mine eyes be packing with my heart,
And called them blind and dusky spectacles,
For losing ken of Albion's wished coast.
How often have I tempted Suffolk's tongue,
The agent of thy foul inconstancy,   120
To sit and witch me, as Ascanius did,
When he to madding Dido would unfold
His father's acts, commenced in burning Troy!
Am I not witched like her? or thou not false like him?
Ay me, I can no more! die, Margaret!   125
For Henry weeps that thou dost live so long.

Noise within. Enter Warwick, [Salisbury,] and many
Commons.

   War. It is reported, mighty sovereign,
That good Duke Humphrey traitorously is murdered
By Suffolk and the Cardinal Beaufort's means.
The commons, like an angry hive of bees   130
That want their leader, scatter up and down
And care not who they sting in his revenge.
Myself have calmed their spleenful mutiny

134. **order:** process.
141. **stay:** comfort; allay.
147. **Fain:** gladly; **paly:** pale.
152. **obsequies:** funeral observances; death rites.
153. **dead and earthy:** as lifeless as earth.

Until they hear the order of his death.

King. That he is dead, good Warwick, 'tis too true;   135
But how he died God knows, not Henry.
Enter his chamber, view his breathless corpse,
And comment then upon his sudden death.

War. That shall I do, my Liege. Stay, Salisbury,
With the rude multitude till I return.   [*Exit.*]   140

King. O Thou that judgest all things, stay my
          thoughts,
My thoughts, that labor to persuade my soul
Some violent hands were laid on Humphrey's life!
If my suspect be false, forgive me, God;   145
For judgment only doth belong to Thee.
Fain would I go to chafe his paly lips
With twenty thousand kisses, and to drain
Upon his face an ocean of salt tears,
To tell my love unto his dumb, deaf trunk   150
And with my fingers feel his hand unfeeling:
But all in vain are these mean obsequies;
And to survey his dead and earthy image,
What were it but to make my sorrow greater?

[*Enter Warwick and others, bearing Gloucester's
          body on a bed.*]

War. Come hither, gracious sovereign, view this   155
          body.

King. That is to see how deep my grave is made;
For with his soul fled all my worldly solace,
For seeing him I see my life in death.

War. As surely as my soul intends to live   160

161. **that dread King:** Jesus Christ; **state:** i.e., state of sin.

166. **instance:** proof; reason.

168. **timely-parted:** departed by natural means; dead of natural causes; **ghost:** corpse.

170. **Being all descended:** i.e., all blood having descended.

172. **aidance:** aid.

184. **lodged:** laid flat.

With that dread King that took our state upon Him
To free us from His Father's wrathful curse.
I do believe that violent hands were laid
Upon the life of this thrice-famed Duke.

 Suf. A dreadful oath, sworn with a solemn tongue! 165
What instance gives Lord Warwick for his vow?

 War. See how the blood is settled in his face.
Oft have I seen a timely-parted ghost,
Of ashy semblance, meager, pale, and bloodless,
Being all descended to the laboring heart, 170
Who, in the conflict that it holds with death,
Attracts the same for aidance 'gainst the enemy;
Which with the heart there cools and ne'er returneth
To blush and beautify the cheek again.
But see, his face is black and full of blood, 175
His eyeballs further out than when he lived,
Staring full ghastly like a strangled man;
His hair upreared, his nostrils stretched with struggling,
His hands abroad displayed, as one that grasped 180
And tugged for life and was by strength subdued.
Look, on the sheets his hair, you see, is sticking;
His well-proportioned beard made rough and rugged,
Like to the summer's corn by tempest lodged.
It cannot be but he was murdered here: 185
The least of all these signs were probable.

 Suf. Why, Warwick, who should do the Duke to
  death?
Myself and Beaufort had him in protection;
And we, I hope, sir, are no murderers. 190

193. **keep:** guard.
194. **like:** likely.
196. **belike:** perhaps.
197. **timeless:** untimely.
199. **fast:** near.
201. **puttock:** kite; a bird of prey.
216. **contumelious:** insolent.
217. **controller:** critic.

War. But both of you were vowed Duke Hum-
    phrey's foes,
And you, forsooth, had the good Duke to keep.
'Tis like you would not feast him like a friend;
And 'tis well seen he found an enemy.   195

    Queen. Then you, belike, suspect these noblemen
As guilty of Duke Humphrey's timeless death.

    War. Who finds the heifer dead and bleeding fresh,
And sees fast by a butcher with an ax,
But will suspect 'twas he that made the slaughter?   200
Who finds the partridge in the puttock's nest
But may imagine how the bird was dead,
Although the kite soar with unbloodied beak?
Even so suspicious is this tragedy.

    Queen. Are you the butcher, Suffolk? Where's your   205
    knife?
Is Beaufort termed a kite? Where are his talons?

    Suf. I wear no knife to slaughter sleeping men;
But here's a vengeful sword, rusted with ease,
That shall be scoured in his rancorous heart   210
That slanders me with murder's crimson badge.
Say, if thou darest, proud lord of Warwickshire,
That I am faulty in Duke Humphrey's death.
        [*Exeunt Cardinal, Somerset, and others.*]

    War. What dares not Warwick, if false Suffolk dare
    him?   215

    Queen. He dares not calm his contumelious spirit,
Nor cease to be an arrogant controller,
Though Suffolk dare him twenty thousand times.

    War. Madam, be still; with reverence may I say,
For every word you speak in his behalf   220

226. **graft:** graffed; grafted.

228. **bucklers:** protects, as with a shield (buckler).

230. **Quitting:** ridding.

237. **hire:** salary; earned reward.

242. **cope:** encounter.

Is slander to your royal dignity.

   Suf. Blunt-witted lord, ignoble in demeanor!
If ever lady wronged her lord so much,
Thy mother took into her blameful bed
Some stern untutored churl, and noble stock   225
Was graft with crab-tree slip; whose fruit thou art
And never of the Nevilles' noble race.

   War. But that the guilt of murder bucklers thee,
And I should rob the deathsman of his fee,
Quitting thee thereby of ten thousand shames,   230
And that my sovereign's presence makes me mild,
I would, false murd'rous coward, on thy knee
Make thee beg pardon for thy passed speech
And say it was thy mother that thou meantst,
That thou thyself wast born in bastardy;   235
And, after all this fearful homage done,
Give thee thy hire and send thy soul to hell,
Pernicious bloodsucker of sleeping men!

   Suf. Thou shalt be waking while I shed thy blood,
If from this presence thou darest go with me.   240

   War. Away even now, or I will drag thee hence.
Unworthy though thou art, I'll cope with thee
And do some service to Duke Humphrey's ghost.
                 Exeunt [*Suffolk and Warwick*].

   King. What stronger breastplate than a heart un-
      tainted!   245
Thrice is he armed that hath his quarrel just,
And he but naked, though locked up in steel,
Whose conscience with injustice is corrupted.
                    A noise within.

   Queen. What noise is this?

266. stubborn: rebellious.

*Enter Suffolk and Warwick, with their weapons
drawn.*

King. Why, how now, lords! your wrathful weapons 250
  drawn
Here in our presence! Dare you be so bold?
Why, what tumultuous clamor have we here?
  Suf. The trait'rous Warwick with the men of Bury
Set all upon me, mighty sovereign.   255
  Sal. [*To the Commons, entering*] Sirs, stand apart;
    the King shall know your mind.—
Dread lord, the commons send you word by me,
Unless Lord Suffolk straight be done to death,
Or banished fair England's territories,   260
They will by violence tear him from your palace
And torture him with grievous ling'ring death.
They say, by him the good Duke Humphrey died;
They say, in him they fear your Highness' death;
And mere instinct of love and loyalty,   265
Free from a stubborn opposite intent,
As being thought to contradict your liking,
Makes them thus forward in his banishment.
They say, in care of your most royal person,
That if your Highness should intend to sleep,   270
And charge that no man should disturb your rest
In pain of your dislike or pain of death,
Yet, notwithstanding such a strait edict,
Were there a serpent seen, with forked tongue,
That slily glided toward your Majesty,   275
It were but necessary you were waked,

277. **suffered:** permitted.
278. **mortal:** deadly.
280. **whe'er:** whether.
281. **fell:** deadly.
287. **like:** likely; **hinds:** rustics; menials.
290. **quaint:** clever.
293. **sort of tinkers:** gang of plebeians.
298. **cited:** urged.

Lest, being suffered in that harmful slumber,
The mortal worm might make the sleep eternal;
And therefore do they cry, though you forbid,
That they will guard you, whe'er you will or no,   280
From such fell serpents as false Suffolk is,
With whose envenomed and fatal sting
Your loving uncle, twenty times his worth,
They say, is shamefully bereft of life.

  Com. [*Within*] An answer from the King, my lord 285
of Salisbury!

  Suf. 'Tis like the commons, rude unpolished hinds,
Could send such message to their sovereign:
But you, my lord, were glad to be employed,
To show how quaint an orator you are.   290
But all the honor Salisbury hath won
Is that he was the lord ambassador
Sent from a sort of tinkers to the King.

  Com. [*Within*] An answer from the King, or we will
all break in!   295

  King. Go, Salisbury, and tell them all from me,
I thank them for their tender loving care;
And had I not been cited so by them,
Yet did I purpose as they do entreat;
For, sure, my thoughts do hourly prophesy   300
Mischance unto my state by Suffolk's means:
And therefore, by His majesty I swear,
Whose far unworthy deputy I am,
He shall not breathe infection in this air
But three days longer, on the pain of death.   305
                             [*Exit Salisbury.*]

  Queen. O Henry, let me plead for gentle Suffolk!

321. **the Devil make a third:** alluding to the proverb "There cannot lightly [easily] come a worse except the Devil come himself."

324. **heavy:** sorrowful.

330. **mandrake's groan:** the mandrake (*Mandragora officinarum*) has a forked root that resembles a man. It was a common belief that the plant shrieked when uprooted and that the sound killed whoever was responsible.

331. **bitter-searching:** searching the depths of bitterness.

332. **curst:** bitter; baneful.

"Lean-faced Envy" in her cave. From Gabriele Simeoni, *La vita et Metamorfoseo d'Ovidio* (1559).

King. Ungentle queen, to call him gentle Suffolk!
No more, I say: if thou dost plead for him,
Thou wilt but add increase unto my wrath.
Had I but said, I would have kept my word,   310
But when I swear, it is irrevocable.
[*To Suffolk*] If, after three days' space, thou here
      beest found
On any ground that I am ruler of,
The world shall not be ransom for thy life.   315
Come, Warwick, come, good Warwick, go with me:
I have great matters to impart to thee.
                        Exeunt [all but Queen and Suffolk].
    Queen. Mischance and sorrow go along with you!
Heart's discontent and sour affliction
Be playfellows to keep you company!   320
There's two of you; the Devil make a third!
And threefold vengeance tend upon your steps!
    Suf. Cease, gentle queen, these execrations,
And let thy Suffolk take his heavy leave.
    Queen. Fie, coward woman and soft-hearted   325
      wretch!
Hast thou not spirit to curse thine enemy?
    Suf. A plague upon them! wherefore should I curse
      them?
Would curses kill, as doth the mandrake's groan,   330
I would invent as bitter-searching terms,
As curst, as harsh and horrible to hear,
Delivered strongly through my fixed teeth,
With full as many signs of deadly hate,
As lean-faced Envy in her loathsome cave.   335
My tongue should stumble in mine earnest words;

338. **an end:** on end.

343. **cypress trees:** traditionally associated with death and general ill fortune.

344. **chiefest prospect:** best view.

345. **smart:** painful.

347. **consort:** musical company.

354. **leave:** cease to do so.

364. **monuments:** memorials.

366. **seal:** impression.

Mine eyes should sparkle like the beaten flint;
Mine hair be fixed an end, as one distract;
Ay, every joint should seem to curse and ban.
And even now my burdened heart would break,   340
Should I not curse them. Poison be their drink!
Gall, worse than gall, the daintiest that they taste!
Their sweetest shade a grove of cypress trees!
Their chiefest prospect murd'ring basilisks!
Their softest touch as smart as lizards' stings!   345
Their music frightful as the serpent's hiss,
And boding screech owls make the consort full!
All the foul terrors in dark-seated hell—
   Queen. Enough, sweet Suffolk: thou tormentst thy-
    self;   350
And these dread curses, like the sun 'gainst glass,
Or like an overcharged gun, recoil
And turns the force of them upon thyself.
   Suf. You bade me ban, and will you bid me leave?
Now, by the ground that I am banished from,   355
Well could I curse away a winter's night,
Though standing naked on a mountain top,
Where biting cold would never let grass grow,
And think it but a minute spent in sport.
   Queen. Oh, let me entreat thee cease. Give me thy   360
    hand,
That I may dew it with my mournful tears;
Nor let the rain of Heaven wet this place,
To wash away my woeful monuments.
Oh, could this kiss be printed in thy hand,   365
That thou mightst think upon these by the seal,

372. **repeal:** recall.

373. **Adventure:** dare.

374. **banished I am, if but from thee:** i.e., I am banished if we are parted. The love between the Queen and Suffolk is unhistorical. Actually Suffolk was much older than Margaret, who was a close friend of his wife.

378. **Loather:** more reluctant.

386. **several:** separate; individual.

388. **joy:** enjoy.

Through whom a thousand sighs are breathed for
　　thee!
So, get thee gone, that I may know my grief:
'Tis but surmised whiles thou art standing by,　　　370
As one that surfeits thinking on a want.
I will repeal thee, or, be well assured,
Adventure to be banished myself:
And banished I am, if but from thee.
Go: speak not to me; even now be gone.　　　375
Oh, go not yet! Even thus two friends condemned
Embrace and kiss and take ten thousand leaves,
Loather a hundred times to part than die.
Yet now farewell; and farewell life with thee!

　　Suf. Thus is poor Suffolk ten times banished;　380
Once by the King, and three times thrice by thee.
'Tis not the land I care for, wert thou thence;
A wilderness is populous enough,
So Suffolk had thy heavenly company:
For where thou art, there is the world itself,　　385
With every several pleasure in the world,
And where thou art not, desolation.
I can no more: live thou to joy thy life;
Myself no joy in nought but that thou livest.

　　　　　　Enter Vaux.

　　Queen. Whither goes Vaux so fast? What news, I　390
　　prithee?
　　Vaux. To signify unto His Majesty
That Cardinal Beaufort is at point of death;
For suddenly a grievous sickness took him,

404. what is this world: what a world this is.

405. an hour's poor loss: i.e., the Cardinal's loss of the brief span of life left to him.

408. southern clouds: the South was considered the source of rain and fog.

423. lived: would live.

That makes him gasp and stare and catch the air,   395
Blaspheming God and cursing men on earth.
Sometime he talks as if Duke Humphrey's ghost
Were by his side; sometime he calls the King
And whispers to his pillow as to him
The secrets of his overcharged soul: 400
And I am sent to tell His Majesty
That even now he cries aloud for him.

    Queen. Go tell this heavy message to the King.

                              Exit [*Vaux*].

Ay me! what is this world! What news are these!
But wherefore grieve I at an hour's poor loss,   405
Omitting Suffolk's exile, my soul's treasure?
Why only, Suffolk, mourn I not for thee,
And with the southern clouds contend in tears,
Theirs for the earth's increase, mine for my sorrows?
Now get thee hence: the King, thou knowst, is coming;   410
If thou be found by me, thou art but dead.

    Suf. If I depart from thee, I cannot live;
And in thy sight to die, what were it else
But like a pleasant slumber in thy lap?
Here could I breathe my soul into the air,   415
As mild and gentle as the cradle babe
Dying with mother's dug between its lips:
Where, from thy sight, I should be raging mad,
And cry out for thee to close up mine eyes,
To have thee with thy lips to stop my mouth.   420
So shouldst thou either turn my flying soul,
Or I should breathe it so into thy body,
And then it lived in sweet Elysium.
To die by thee were but to die in jest;

427. **fretful corrosive:** remedy that chafes and corrodes; hence, a painful cure.

431. **Iris:** messenger; literally, the messenger of the gods.

434. **cask:** casket.

[III.iii.] The King, Salisbury, and Warwick visit the Cardinal's deathbed. The dying man's ravings reveal his guilt and his fear of death. The King prays to Heaven to have mercy on the wretch, but Warwick sees in the horror of his death a judgment on the man's sins.

From thee to die were torture more than death. 425
Oh, let me stay, befall what may befall!
  Queen. Away! though parting be a fretful corrosive,
It is applied to a deathful wound.
To France, sweet Suffolk. Let me hear from thee;
For wheresoe'er thou art in this world's globe, 430
I'll have an Iris that shall find thee out.
  Suf. I go.
  Queen. And take my heart with thee.
  Suf. A jewel, locked into the woefull'st cask
That ever did contain a thing of worth. 435
Even as a splitted bark, so sunder we:
This way fall I to death.
  Queen.   This way for me.
                       Exeunt [severally].

[Scene III. London. Cardinal Beaufort's
bedchamber.]

*Enter the King, Salisbury, and Warwick to the
Cardinal in bed.*

  King. How fares my lord? Speak, Beaufort, to thy
    sovereign.
  Car. If thou beest Death, I'll give thee England's
    treasure,
Enough to purchase such another island, 5
So thou wilt let me live and feel no pain.
  King. Ah, what a sign it is of evil life,

27. grin: grimace.

Where death's approach is seen so terrible!
  War. Beaufort, it is thy sovereign speaks to thee.
  Car. Bring me unto my trial when you will.   10
Died he not in his bed? Where should he die?
Can I make men live, whe'er they will or no?
Oh, torture me no more! I will confess.
Alive again? Then show me where he is:
I'll give a thousand pound to look upon him.   15
He hath no eyes, the dust hath blinded them.
Comb down his hair: look, look! it stands upright,
Like lime-twigs set to catch my winged soul.
Give me some drink; and bid the apothecary
Bring the strong poison that I bought of him.   20
  King. O Thou eternal mover of the heavens,
Look with a gentle eye upon this wretch!
Oh, beat away the busy meddling fiend
That lays strong siege unto this wretch's soul,
And from his bosom purge this black despair!   25
  War. See, how the pangs of death do make him
    grin!
  Sal. Disturb him not; let him pass peaceably.
  King. Peace to his soul, if God's good pleasure be!
Lord Card'nal, if thou thinkst on Heaven's bliss,   30
Hold up thy hand, make signal of thy hope.
He dies and makes no sign. O God, forgive him!
  War. So bad a death argues a monstrous life.
  King. Forbear to judge, for we are sinners all.
Close up his eyes and draw the curtain close;   35
And let us all to meditation.

                              Exeunt.

THE SECOND PART
OF
HENRY THE SIXTH

ACT IV

[IV.i.] Off the coast of Kent, Suffolk and other prisoners are threatened with death by a ship's crew who have captured them. Suffolk finds himself the prize of Walter (pronounced "Water") Whitmore, whose name recalls to him the prediction that he will die by water. Whitmore is implacable, and, after hearing a recital of his misdeeds, Suffolk is beheaded. One of the gentlemen who has arranged for ransom takes the body to the Queen.

—————

1. **gaudy:** brilliant; **blabbing:** revealing everything; allowing nothing to be concealed; **remorseful:** compassionate.

3. **jades:** nags. Night's chariot is described by contemporary writers as drawn by horses or dragons.

6. **Clip:** embrace.

7. **contagious darkness:** the dank night air was considered particularly favorable to contagion.

11. **discolored:** i.e., by the spilled blood.

13. **boot:** profit.

[ACT IV]

[Scene I. The coast of Kent.]

Alarum. Fight at sea. Ordnance goes off. Enter Lieutenant, [a Master, a Master's Mate, Walter Whitmore,] and others; [with them] Suffolk, [and others, prisoners].

Lieut. The gaudy, blabbing, and remorseful day
Is crept into the bosom of the sea;
And now loud-howling wolves arouse the jades
That drag the tragic melancholy Night;
Who, with their drowsy, slow, and flagging wings,   5
Clip dead men's graves and from their misty jaws
Breathe foul contagious darkness in the air.
Therefore bring forth the soldiers of our prize;
For, whilst our pinnace anchors in the Downs,
Here shall they make their ransom on the sand   10
Or with their blood stain this discolored shore.
Master, this prisoner freely give I thee;
And thou, that art his mate, make boot of this:
The other, Walter Whitmore, is thy share.
1. Gent. What is my ransom, Master? let me know.   15

22. **port:** general behavior and style of living; cf. deportment.

25. **counterpoised:** balanced.

29–30. **laying the prize aboard:** i.e., boarding and seizing the prize.

34. **George:** likeness of St. George, part of the insignia of the Order of the Garter.

41. **water:** Walter (spelled without the *l* in the Quarto) was pronounced like **water.**

43. **Gualtier:** the old French form of the name.

Mast. A thousand crowns, or else lay down your
    head.

Mate. And so much shall you give, or off goes
    yours.

Lieut. What, think you much to pay two thousand   20
    crowns,
And bear the name and port of gentlemen?
Cut both the villains' throats; for die you shall:
The lives of those which we have lost in fight
Be counterpoised with such a petty sum!   25

    1. Gent. I'll give it, sir; and therefore spare my life.

    2. Gent. And so will I, and write home for it
    straight.

    Whit. [*To Suffolk*] I lost mine eye in laying the
    prize aboard,   30
And therefore, to revenge it, shalt thou die;
And so should these, if I might have my will.

    Lieut. Be not so rash: take ransom, let him live.

    Suf. Look on my George: I am a gentleman.
Rate me at what thou wilt, thou shalt be paid.   35

    Whit. And so am I: my name is Walter Whitmore.
How now! why starts thou? What, doth death affright?

    Suf. Thy name affrights me, in whose sound is
    death.
A cunning man did calculate my birth   40
And told me that by water I should die.
Yet let not this make thee be bloody-minded:
Thy name is Gualtier, being rightly sounded.

    Whit. Gualtier or Walter, which it is, I care not:
Never yet did base dishonor blur our name,   45
But with our sword we wiped away the blot;

48. **arms:** coat of arms.

58. **jaded:** mean; contemptible.

60. **footcloth:** ornamental trappings for an animal.

65. **crestfall'n:** humble.

66. **abortive:** unavailing.

67. **voiding lobby:** antechamber.

71. **forlorn:** abandoned; cast off; **swain:** lover (of Queen Margaret).

Therefore, when merchant-like I sell revenge,
Broke be my sword, my arms torn and defaced,
And I proclaimed a coward through the world!

   Suf. Stay, Whitmore, for thy prisoner is a prince,   50
The Duke of Suffolk, William de la Pole.

   Whit. The Duke of Suffolk, muffled up in rags!

   Suf. Ay, but these rags are no part of the Duke:
Jove sometime went disguised, and why not I?

   Lieut. But Jove was never slain, as thou shalt be.   55

   Suf. Obscure and lowly swain, King Henry's blood,
The honorable blood of Lancaster,
Must not be shed by such a jaded groom.
Hast thou not kissed thy hand and held my stirrup?
Bareheaded plodded by my footcloth mule,   60
And thought thee happy when I shook my head?
How often hast thou waited at my cup,
Fed from my trencher, kneeled down at the board,
When I have feasted with Queen Margaret?
Remember it and let it make thee crestfall'n,   65
Ay, and allay this thy abortive pride;
How in our voiding lobby hast thou stood
And duly waited for my coming forth?
This hand of mine hath writ in thy behalf,
And therefore shall it charm thy riotous tongue.   70

   Whit. Speak, captain, shall I stab the forlorn swain?

   Lieut. First let my words stab him, as he hath me.

   Suf. Base slave, thy words are blunt, and so art
     thou.

   Lieut. Convey him hence and on our longboat's side   75
Strike off his head.

   Suf.   Thou darest not, for thy own.

81. **kennel:** variant of "cannel," street gutter; **sink:** sewer.

91. **hags of hell:** i.e., the Furies of mythology.

92. **affy:** betroth.

96. **Sylla:** Lucius Cornelius Sulla (139–78 B.C.), who as dictator of Rome had thousands of citizens murdered.

97. **mother's:** motherland's.

99. **thorough:** through.

101. **surprised:** captured.

107. **guiltless king:** Richard II. Edmund Mortimer had been officially recognized as his heir in default of any children of his own. Since Mortimer died childless, York would be next in line.

108. **encroaching tyranny:** Henry IV's usurpation, maintained by his son and grandson.

Richard II. From John Taylor, *All the Works* (1630).

Lieut. Yes, Pole.

Suf.   Pole!

Lieut.   Pool! Sir Pool! lord!   80
Ay, kennel, puddle, sink; whose filth and dirt
Troubles the silver spring where England drinks.
Now will I dam up this thy yawning mouth
For swallowing the treasure of the realm.
Thy lips that kissed the Queen shall sweep the   85
     ground;
And thou that smiledst at good Duke Humphrey's
     death
Against the senseless winds shalt grin in vain,
Who in contempt shall hiss at thee again.   90
And wedded be thou to the hags of hell,
For daring to affy a mighty lord
Unto the daughter of a worthless king,
Having neither subject, wealth, nor diadem.
By devilish policy art thou grown great,   95
And, like ambitious Sylla, overgorged
With gobbets of thy mother's bleeding heart.
By thee Anjou and Maine were sold to France,
The false revolting Normans thorough thee
Disdain to call us lord, and Picardy   100
Hath slain their governors, surprised our forts,
And sent the ragged soldiers wounded home.
The princely Warwick, and the Nevilles all,
Whose dreadful swords were never drawn in vain,
As hating thee, are rising up in arms: 105
And now the house of York, thrust from the crown
By shameful murder of a guiltless king,
And lofty proud encroaching tyranny,

109. **colors:** standards.

110. **Advance:** raise; **our half-faced sun:** Edward III used rays of the sun emerging from clouds on his banners and standards. York's partisans regarded his descent from Edward III as nearer than that of the house of Lancaster.

111. **Invitis nubibus:** in spite of the clouds (not a motto associated with the device, however).

113. **reproach and beggary:** shameful beggary.

120. **Bargulus:** a character mentioned in Cicero's *Offices.*

129. **Gelidus timor occupat artus:** "cold fear seizes my limbs"; Shakespeare's adaptation of a line from the *Aeneid* (vii.446).

132. **stoop:** submit.

Burns with revenging fire; whose hopeful colors
Advance our half-faced sun, striving to shine,   110
Under the which is writ, *"Invitis nubibus."*
The commons here in Kent are up in arms:
And, to conclude, reproach and beggary
Is crept into the palace of our king,
And all by thee. Away! convey him hence.   115
   Suf. Oh, that I were a god, to shoot forth thunder
Upon these paltry, servile, abject drudges!
Small things make base men proud: this villain here,
Being captain of a pinnace, threatens more
Than Bargulus, the strong Illyrian pirate.   120
Drones suck not eagles' blood but rob beehives.
It is impossible that I should die
By such a lowly vassal as thyself.
Thy words move rage and not remorse in me.
I go of message from the Queen to France: 125
I charge thee waft me safely cross the Channel.
   Lieut. Walter—
   Whit. Come, Suffolk, I must waft thee to thy death.
   Suf. Gelidus timor occupat artus: it is thee I fear.
   Whit. Thou shalt have cause to fear before I leave   130
    thee.
What, are ye daunted now? Now will ye stoop?
   1. Gent. My gracious lord, entreat him, speak him
    fair.
   Suf. Suffolk's imperial tongue is stern and rough,   135
Used to command, untaught to plead for favor.
Far be it we should honor such as these
With humble suit: no, rather let my head
Stoop to the block than these knees bow to any

148. **bezonians:** literally, beggars (from Italian *bisógno*, need); hence, base fellows.

149. **sworder:** swordsman.

150. **Tully:** the Elizabethan name for Marcus Tullius Cicero, who was murdered by order of Mark Antony; **Brutus:** the hint that Brutus was the bastard son of Julius Caesar derives from Plutarch.

152. **Pompey the Great:** actually slain in Egypt. The word **islanders** may result from the fact that Pompey was killed on the advice of Theodotus, described by Plutarch as from the Isle of Chios.

Save to the God of Heaven and to my king;   140
And sooner dance upon a bloody pole
Than stand uncovered to the vulgar groom.
True nobility is exempt from fear:
More can I bear than you dare execute.
    Lieut. Hale him away, and let him talk no more.   145
    Suf. Come, soldiers, show what cruelty ye can,
That this my death may never be forgot!
Great men oft die by vile bezonians:
A Roman sworder and banditto slave
Murdered sweet Tully; Brutus' bastard hand   150
Stabbed Julius Caesar, savage islanders
Pompey the Great; and Suffolk dies by pirates.
        Exeunt Whitmore [and others] with Suffolk.
    Lieut. And as for these whose ransom we have set,
It is our pleasure one of them depart:
Therefore come you with us and let him go.   155
        Exeunt [all but the First Gentleman].

    Enter Whitmore with [Suffolk's] body.

    Whit. There let his head and lifeless body lie,
Until the Queen his mistress bury it.   *Exit.*
    1. Gent. O barbarous and bloody spectacle!
His body will I bear unto the King:
If he revenge it not, yet will his friends;   160
So will the Queen, that living held him dear.
        Exit [with the body].

[IV.ii.] Jack Cade, who claims to be one John Mortimer, has led a rabble to the outskirts of London. His program promises free food and drink for all, property held in common, and death to all lawyers. A clerk is hanged because he confesses his literacy. Sir Humphrey Stafford and his brother appeal to the rebels to submit and enjoy the King's mercy. Cade defies the Staffords, who threaten to attack them with the royal forces and to have all Cade's followers declared traitors.

12–3. **leather aprons:** worn by artisans.
16. **it is said:** see I Cor. 7:20 (Geneva Bible). The injunction was repeated in the official *Book of Homilies* that the Church of England commanded to be read at Sunday services.
18. **magistrates:** administrators of government.

[Scene II. Blackheath.]

Enter [George] Bevis and John Holland.

Bevis. Come, and get thee a sword, though made of
a lath: they have been up these two days.

Holl. They have the more need to sleep now, then.

Bevis. I tell thee, Jack Cade the clothier means to
dress the commonwealth, and turn it, and set a new   5
nap upon it.

Holl. So he had need, for 'tis threadbare. Well, I
say it was never merry world in England since gentlemen came up.

Bevis. O miserable age! virtue is not regarded in   10
handicraftsmen.

Holl. The nobility think scorn to go in leather
aprons.

Bevis. Nay, more, the King's Council are no good
workmen.   15

Holl. True! and yet it is said, labor in thy vocation;
which is as much to say as, let the magistrates be laboring men; and therefore should we be magistrates.

Bevis. Thou hast hit it; for there's no better sign of
a brave mind than a hard hand.   20

Holl. I see them! I see them! There's Best's son,
the tanner of Wingham—

Bevis. He shall have the skins of our enemies, to
make dog's leather of.

Holl. And Dick the butcher—   25

29. Argo: corruption of Latin *ergo*, "therefore," a learned word often placed in the mouths of ignorant clowns; **thread of life:** the Fates of classical mythology controlled human life by means of a thread that one spun, another measured, and a third cut to the predetermined length.

31. We: the royal plural.

32. father: i.e., Edmund Mortimer, so he claimed.

33. cade: barrel.

35. For our enemies shall fall before us: compare Latin *cado*, "to fall," upon which Cade here makes a pun.

48. furred pack: i.e., knapsack made of skin; **bucks:** laundry.

52. the cage: jail.

The Fates, with the thread of human destiny. From Vincenzo Cartari, *Imagini de i dei de gli antichi* (1587).

Bevis. Then is sin struck down like an ox and in-
iquity's throat cut like a calf.

Holl. And Smith the weaver—

Bevis. Argo, their thread of life is spun.

Holl. Come, come, let's fall in with them.   3(

Drum. Enter Cade, Dick Butcher, Smith the Weaver,
and a Sawyer, with infinite numbers.

Cade. We John Cade, so termed of our supposed
father—

Dick. [*Aside*] Or rather, of stealing a cade of her-
rings.

Cade. For our enemies shall fall before us, inspired   35
with the spirit of putting down kings and princes—
Command silence.

Dick. Silence!

Cade. My father was a Mortimer—

Dick. [*Aside*] He was an honest man, and a good   40
bricklayer.

Cade. My mother a Plantagenet—

Dick. [*Aside*] I knew her well: she was a midwife.

Cade. My wife descended of the Lacies—

Dick. [*Aside*] She was, indeed, a peddler's daugh-   45
ter, and sold many laces.

Smith. [*Aside*] But now of late, not able to travel
with her furred pack, she washes bucks here at home.

Cade. Therefore am I of an honorable house.

Dick. [*Aside*] Ay, by my faith, the field is honor-   50
able; and there was he born, under a hedge, for his
father had never a house but the cage.

54. **'A:** he; **beggary is valiant:** able-bodied men who wandered and begged for a living were called "sturdy" or "valiant" beggars in statutes and official documents of the time.

60. **of proof:** (1) designed to resist penetration; (2) well tried; old and shabby.

65–6. **three-hooped pot:** a container ringed with three metal bands. Cade intends that the current price will prevail for a container holding more than three times as much liquor.

67. **small beer:** weak beer; **in common:** owned in common.

68. **Cheapside:** the main street of the market area of London, containing many shops.

72. **on my score:** at my expense. Accounts were kept by scoring a stick.

73. **livery:** uniform.

80–1. **seal once to a thing:** referring, probably, to having signed articles of apprenticeship.

Cade. Valiant I am.

Smith. [*Aside*] 'A must needs; for beggary is valiant.

Cade. I am able to endure much.   55

Dick. [*Aside*] No question of that; for I have seen
him whipped three market days together.

Cade. I fear neither sword nor fire.

Smith [*Aside*] He need not fear the sword; for his
coat is of proof.   60

Dick. [*Aside*] But methinks he should stand in fear
of fire, being burnt i' the hand for stealing of sheep.

Cade. Be brave, then; for your captain is brave and
vows reformation. There shall be in England seven
halfpenny loaves sold for a penny; the three-hooped   65
pot shall have ten hoops, and I will make it felony to
drink small beer. All the realm shall be in common;
and in Cheapside shall my palfry go to grass: and
when I am King, as King I will be—

All. God save your Majesty!   70

Cade. I thank you, good people: there shall be no
money: all shall eat and drink on my score; and I will
apparel them all in one livery, that they may agree
like brothers and worship me their lord.

Dick. The first thing we do, let's kill all the lawyers.   75

Cade. Nay, that I mean to do. Is not this a lament-
able thing, that of the skin of an innocent lamb should
be made parchment? that parchment, being scribbled
o'er, should undo a man? Some say the bee stings;
but I say, 'tis the bee's wax: for I did but seal once to   80
a thing, and I was never mine own man since. How
now! who's there?

84. **accompt:** account.

86. **setting of boys' copies:** giving schoolboys copy on which to practice their penmanship.

88. **books ... with red letters:** primers with red initial letters.

91–2. **make obligations:** draw up legal bonds in the proper form; **court hand:** the distinctive style of writing used in the law courts and by government officials.

93. **proper:** fine; exemplary; **of:** on.

97. **Emmanuel:** since the name literally means "God with us," it was placed at the top of letters as an indication of the writer's piety.

100. **Let me alone:** leave this matter to me; **Dost thou use to write:** are you in the habit of writing.

*Enter [some, bringing forward the] Clerk [of
Chatham].*

Smith. The clerk of Chatham: he can write and
read and cast accompt.

Cade. Oh, monstrous!   85

Smith. We took him setting of boys' copies.

Cade. Here's a villain!

Smith. Has a book in his pocket with red letters
in 't.

Cade. Nay, then, he is a conjurer.   90

Dick. Nay, he can make obligations, and write court
hand.

Cade. I am sorry for 't. The man is a proper man, of
mine honor: unless I find him guilty, he shall not die.
Come hither, sirrah, I must examine thee: what is thy   95
name?

Clerk. Emmanuel.

Dick. They use to write it on the top of letters:
'twill go hard with you.

Cade. Let me alone. Dost thou use to write thy   100
name? or hast thou a mark to thyself, like an honest
plain-dealing man?

Clerk. Sir, I thank God, I have been so well brought
up that I can write my name.

All. He hath confessed: away with him! He's a   105
villain and a traitor.

Cade. Away with him, I say! Hang him with his pen
and inkhorn about his neck. *Exit one with the Clerk.*

110. particular: private, in humorous contrast to general.

112. hard: near.

119. have at him: let him defend himself.

120. hinds: menials.

123. revolt: turn about; desert Cade.

126. pass: care.

131. shearman: a shearer of woolen cloth during the manufacturing process.

132. Adam was a gardener: during Wat Tyler's rebellion in 1381, from which Shakespeare took some details for Cade's uprising, a verse attributed to John Ball became current: "When Adam delved and Eve span,/ Who was then the gentleman?"

Adam with a gardener's spade. From a manuscript commonplace book (ca. 1608). (Folger MS. V.b. 232.)

Enter Michael.

Mich. Where's our general?

Cade. Here I am, thou particular fellow.   110

Mich. Fly, fly, fly! Sir Humphrey Stafford and his
brother are hard by, with the King's forces.

Cade. Stand, villain, stand, or I'll fell thee down.
He shall be encountered with a man as good as himself. He is but a knight, is 'a?   115

Mich. No.

Cade. To equal him, I will make myself a knight
presently. [*Kneels*] Rise up, Sir John Mortimer.
[*Rises*] Now have at him!

*Enter Sir Humphrey Stafford and his Brother, with
drum and soldiers.*

Staff. Rebellious hinds, the filth and scum of Kent,   120
Marked for the gallows, lay your weapons down:
Home to your cottages, forsake this groom.
The King is merciful, if you revolt.

Bro. But angry, wrathful, and inclined to blood,
If you go forward: therefore yield, or die.   125

Cade. As for these silken-coated slaves, I pass not;
It is to you, good people, that I speak,
Over whom, in time to come, I hope to reign;
For I am rightful heir unto the crown.

Staff. Villain, thy father was a plasterer,   130
And thou thyself a shearman, art thou not?

Cade. And Adam was a gardener.

156. sirrah: a form of address reserved for inferiors.

158. span-counter: a game of tossing counters (slugs), the object being to place one's own within a handspan of the opponent's; **crowns:** (1) coins; (2) heads.

163. mained: a spelling of "maimed"; **fain:** forced.

163–64. puissance: power.

Bro. And what of that?

Cade. Marry, this: Edmund Mortimer, Earl of
    March,   135

Married the Duke of Clarence' daughter, did he not?

Staff. Ay, sir.

Cade. By her he had two children at one birth.

Bro. That's false.

Cade. Ay, there's the question; but I say, 'tis true. 140
The elder of them, being put to nurse,
Was by a beggarwoman stol'n away;
And, ignorant of his birth and parentage,
Became a bricklayer when he came to age.
His son am I: deny it, if you can.   145

Dick. Nay, 'tis too true; therefore he shall be King.

Smith. Sir, he made a chimney in my father's house,
and the bricks are alive at this day to testify it: therefore deny it not.

Staff. And will you credit this base drudge's words, 150
That speaks he knows not what?

All. Ay, marry, will we: therefore get ye gone.

Bro. Jack Cade, the Duke of York hath taught you
this.

Cade. [*Aside*] He lies, for I invented it myself.— 155
Go to, sirrah, tell the King from me, that, for his
father's sake, Henry the Fifth, in whose time boys
went to span-counter for French crowns, I am content
he shall reign; but I'll be Protector over him.

Dick. And furthermore, we'll have the Lord Say's 160
head for selling the Dukedom of Maine.

Cade. And good reason; for thereby is England
mained and fain to go with a staff, but that my puis-

170. Go to: very well; come on.
185. clouted shoon: hobnailed shoes.

sance holds it up. Fellow kings, I tell you that that
Lord Say hath gelded the commonwealth and made 165
it an eunuch: and more than that, he can speak
French, and therefore he is a traitor.

Staff. Oh, gross and miserable ignorance!

Cade. Nay, answer, if you can: the Frenchmen are
our enemies. Go to, then, I ask but this: can he that 170
speaks with the tongue of an enemy be a good coun-
selor, or no?

All. No, no: and therefore we'll have his head.

Bro. Well, seeing gentle words will not prevail,
Assail them with the army of the King. 175

Staff. Herald, away, and throughout every town
Proclaim them traitors that are up with Cade;
That those which fly before the battle ends
May, even in their wives' and children's sight,
Be hanged up for example at their doors: 180
And you that be the King's friends, follow me.

Exeunt [the two Staffords, and soldiers].

Cade. And you that love the commons, follow me.
Now show yourselves men: 'tis for liberty.
We will not leave one lord, one gentleman:
Spare none but such as go in clouted shoon; 185
For they are thrifty, honest men and such
As would, but that they dare not, take our parts.

Dick. They are all in order and march toward us.

Cade. But then are we in order when we are most
out of order. Come, march forward. 190

Exeunt.

[IV.iii.] Cade's men meet the Staffords in battle and slay them. Cade dons Sir Humphrey's armor and orders the bodies dragged at his horse's heels to London.

▬▬▬▬▬▬▬▬▬▬▬▬▬▬

7. **license:** the eating of meat was forbidden during Lent, and the slaughter of animals was correspondingly controlled.

11. **monument:** trophy.

SD 12. **brigandine:** suit of body armor.

18. **Fear:** doubt; **warrant:** guarantee.

[Scene III. Another part of Blackheath.]

*Alarums to the fight, wherein both the Staffords are
       slain. Enter Cade and the rest.*

Cade. Where's Dick, the butcher of Ashford?
Dick. Here, sir.
Cade. They fell before thee like sheep and oxen,
and thou behavedst thyself as if thou hadst been in
thine own slaughterhouse: therefore thus will I re-   5
ward thee, the Lent shall be as long again as it is;
and thou shalt have a license to kill for a hundred
lacking one.
Dick. I desire no more.
Cade. And, to speak truth, thou deservest no less.   10
This monument of the victory will I bear [*putting on
Sir Humphrey's brigandine*]; and the bodies shall be
dragged at my horse heels till I do come to London,
where we will have the Mayor's sword borne before
us.   15
Dick. If we mean to thrive and do good, break
open the jails and let out the prisoners.
Cade. Fear not that, I warrant thee. Come, let's
march toward London.
                                               Exeunt.

[IV.iv] The Queen grieves over Suffolk's head, as the King and Buckingham consider a message from the rebels. Warned that Cade's rabble have reached Southwark, they retire to the safety of Kenilworth Castle. Lord Say, whom the rebels threaten to kill, resolves to stay in London rather than be an added danger to the King.

[Scene IV. London. The palace.]

Enter the King, with a supplication, and the Queen,
with Suffolk's head; the Duke of Buckingham, and the
Lord Say.

   Queen. Oft have I heard that grief softens the mind,
And makes it fearful and degenerate;
Think therefore on revenge and cease to weep.
But who can cease to weep and look on this?
Here may his head lie on my throbbing breast: 5
But where's the body that I should embrace?
   Buck. What answer makes your Grace to the rebels'
     supplication?
   King. I'll send some holy bishop to entreat;
For God forbid so many simple souls   10
Should perish by the sword! And I myself,
Rather than bloody war shall cut them short,
Will parley with Jack Cade their general.
But stay, I'll read it over once again.
   Queen. Ah, barbarous villains! hath this lovely face   15
Ruled, like a wandering planet, over me,
And could it not enforce them to relent,
That were unworthy to behold the same?
   King. Lord Say, Jack Cade hath sworn to have thy
     head.   20
   Say. Ay, but I hope your Highness shall have his.
   King. How now, madam!
Still lamenting and mourning for Suffolk's death?

40. **caterpillars:** destructive parasites.
41. **graceless:** wicked.
43. **Killingworth:** Kenilworth Castle, in Warwickshire.
44. **power:** army.

I fear me, love, if that I had been dead,
Thou wouldst not have mourned so much for me.   25
    Queen. No, my love, I should not mourn but die for
      thee.

Enter a Messenger.

    King. How now! what news? Why comest thou in
      such haste?
    Mess. The rebels are in Southwark: fly, my lord!   30
Jack Cade proclaims himself Lord Mortimer,
Descended from the Duke of Clarence' house,
And calls your Grace usurper openly,
And vows to crown himself in Westminster.
His army is a ragged multitude   35
Of hinds and peasants, rude and merciless.
Sir Humphrey Stafford and his brother's death
Hath given them heart and courage to proceed.
All scholars, lawyers, courtiers, gentlemen,
They call false caterpillars and intend their death.   40
    King. Oh, graceless men! they know not what they
      do.
    Buck. My gracious lord, retire to Killingworth,
Until a power be raised to put them down.
    Queen. Ah, were the Duke of Suffolk now alive,   45
These Kentish rebels would be soon appeased!
    King. Lord Say, the traitors hate thee;
Therefore away with us to Killingworth.
    Say. So might your Grace's person be in danger.
The sight of me is odious in their eyes;   50

54. **citizens:** substantial burghers.
57. **spoil:** loot.

▪▪▪

[IV.v.] Lord Scales at the Tower of London hears that Cade has taken London Bridge and that the Mayor requests aid in defending the city against the rebels. Scales promises all the aid he can spare.

And therefore in this city will I stay
And live alone as secret as I may.

Enter another Messenger.

Mess. Jack Cade hath gotten London Bridge.
The citizens fly and forsake their houses.
The rascal people, thirsting after prey,   55
Join with the traitor, and they jointly swear
To spoil the city and your royal court.
    Buck. Then linger not, my lord: away, take horse.
    King. Come, Margaret: God, our hope, will succor
    us.   60
    Queen. My hope is gone, now Suffolk is deceased.
    King. [*To Lord Say*] Farewell, my lord: trust not
    the Kentish rebels.
    Buck. Trust nobody, for fear you be betrayed.
    Say. The trust I have is in mine innocence,   65
And therefore am I bold and resolute.

                                          Exeunt.

[Scene V. London. The Tower.]

*Enter Lord Scales upon the Tower, walking. Then
    enter two or three Citizens below.*

Scales. How now! is Jack Cade slain?
    1. Cit. No, my lord, nor likely to be slain; for they
have won the bridge, killing all those that withstand

4. **craves**: requests.

9. **Smithfield**: a market area east of the Tower; **gather head**: assemble forces for battle.

▓▓▓▓▓▓▓▓▓▓▓▓▓▓▓▓▓▓▓▓▓▓▓▓▓▓▓▓▓▓▓▓▓▓▓▓

[IV.vi.] In Cannon Street, Cade strikes his staff on London Stone and proclaims himself, Mortimer, lord of the city. A soldier who addresses him as Jack Cade is executed; Cade insists that henceforth he must be called Lord Mortimer. Hearing of an army gathered at Smithfield, Cade orders London Bridge fired.

▓▓▓▓▓▓▓▓▓▓▓▓▓▓▓▓▓▓▓▓▓▓▓▓▓▓▓▓▓▓

Ent. London Stone: this relic, formerly located in the wall of St. Swithin's Church in Cannon Street, is believed to be a Roman milestone that stood in Agricola's London forum, from which distances were measured along the Roman military roads throughout Britain.

3. **of**: at.

London Stone. An anonymous engraving of unknown date.

them. The Lord Mayor craves aid of your Honor from
the Tower to defend the city from the rebels.   5
  Scales. Such aid as I can spare you shall command;
But I am troubled here with them myself:
The rebels have assayed to win the Tower.
But get you to Smithfield and gather head,
And thither I will send you Matthew Goffe: 10
Fight for your King, your country, and your lives!
And so, farewell, for I must hence again.

                                              Exeunt.

[Scene VI. London. Cannon Street.]

*Enter Jack Cade and the rest, and strikes his staff on
                  London Stone.*

  Cade. Now is Mortimer lord of this city. And here,
sitting upon London Stone, I charge and command
that, of the city's cost, the pissing-conduit run nothing but claret wine this first year of our reign. And
now henceforward it shall be treason for any that   5
calls me other than Lord Mortimer.

                Enter a Soldier, running.

  Sol. Jack Cade! Jack Cade!
  Cade. Knock him down there.   *They kill him.*
  Smith. If this fellow be wise, he'll never call ye Jack
Cade more: I think he hath a very fair warning.   10

[IV.vii.] At Smithfield, Lord Say is brought before Cade. The luckless Lord, accused of a variety of misdeeds, denies the charges and makes such an eloquent defense of himself that even Cade is impressed, but not enough to soften his sentence of beheading. Cade also orders that Say's son-in-law's head be cut off. The rabble set off with the two heads stuck on poles.

▬▬▬▬▬▬▬▬▬▬▬▬

1–2. the Savoy: destroyed during the 1381 rising, when it was a residence of John of Gaunt. It had not been rebuilt by the time of Cade's rebellion, but a hospital was built on the site in 1509 by Henry VII.

The Savoy in 1650. An eighteenth-century engraving after an etching by Wenceslaus Hollar.

Dick. My lord, there's an army gathered together
in Smithfield.

Cade. Come, then, let's go fight with them: but
first, go and set London Bridge on fire; and, if you
can, burn down the Tower too. Come, let's away.   15
                                        Exeunt.

[Scene VII. London. Smithfield.]

*Alarums. Matthew Goffe is slain and all the rest.
Then enter Jack Cade and his company.*

Cade. So, sirs: now go some and pull down the
Savoy. Others to the Inns of Court: down with them
all.

Dick. I have a suit unto your Lordship.

Cade. Be it a lordship, thou shalt have it for that   5
word.

Dick. Only that the laws of England may come out
of your mouth.

Holl. [*Aside*] Mass, 'twill be sore law, then; for he
was thrust in the mouth with a spear, and 'tis not   10
whole yet.

Smith. [*Aside*] Nay, John, it will be stinking law;
for his breath stinks with eating toasted cheese.

Cade. I have thought upon it; it shall be so. Away,
burn all the records of the realm: my mouth shall be   15
the Parliament of England.

Holl. [*Aside*] Then we are like to have biting statutes, unless his teeth be pulled out.

24. **subsidy:** tax assessment voted by Parliament to help the sovereign meet unusual expenses.

26. **say:** a cloth similar to serge, punning on his name; **buckram:** a coarse, stiffened cloth.

29. **Basimecu:** kiss my backside (French *baise mon cul*).

30–31. **Be it known unto thee by these presents:** a formal phrase used at the beginning of legal documents and official declarations.

32. **besom:** broom.

36. **books:** i.e., account books; **score and . . . tally:** accounts were kept by scoring a **tally** (wooden rod) with notches.

37. **King his:** King's.

Cade. And henceforward all things shall be in com-   20
mon.

Enter a Messenger.

Mess. My lord, a prize, a prize! Here's the Lord
Say, which sold the towns in France, he that made us
pay one-and-twenty fifteens, and one shilling to the
pound, the last subsidy.

Enter George [Bevis,] with the Lord Say.

Cade. Well, he shall be beheaded for it ten times.   25
Ah, thou say, thou serge, nay, thou buckram lord!
now art thou within point-blank of our jurisdiction
regal. What canst thou answer to My Majesty for giving up of Normandy unto Mounsieur Basimecu, the
Dauphin of France? Be it known unto thee by these   30
presents, even the presence of Lord Mortimer, that I
am the besom that must sweep the court clean of such
filth as thou art. Thou hast most traitorously corrupted
the youth of the realm in erecting a grammar school:
and whereas, before, our forefathers had no other   35
books but the score and the tally, thou hast caused
printing to be used, and, contrary to the King his
crown and dignity, thou hast built a paper mill. It will
be proved to thy face that thou hast men about thee
that usually talk of a noun and a verb and such abomi-   40
nable words as no Christian ear can endure to hear.
Thou hast appointed justices of peace, to call poor
men before them about matters they were not able to

45. **because they could not read:** if they could read a passage called "neck verse," they could plead "benefit of clergy" and be saved from execution.

52. **hose and doublets:** breeches, stockings, and jackets.

57. **bona terra, mala gens:** good country, bad people.

65. **liberal:** generous.

74. **book:** learning; **preferred me to the King:** won me the King's favor.

answer. Moreover, thou hast put them in prison; and
because they could not read, thou hast hanged them; 45
when, indeed, only for that cause they have been most
worthy to live. Thou dost ride in a footcloth, dost
thou not?

Say. What of that?

Cade. Marry, thou oughtst not to let thy horse wear 50
a cloak, when honester men than thou go in their
hose and doublets.

Dick. And work in their shirt too; as myself, for
example, that am a butcher.

Say. You men of Kent— 55

Dick. What say you of Kent?

Say. Nothing but this: 'tis *bona terra, mala gens*.

Cade. Away with him, away with him! He speaks
Latin.

Say. Hear me but speak, and bear me where you 60
will.

Kent, in the Commentaries Caesar writ,
Is termed the civil'st place of all this isle:
Sweet is the country, because full of riches;
The people liberal, valiant, active, wealthy; 65
Which makes me hope you are not void of pity.
I sold not Maine, I lost not Normandy,
Yet to recover them would lose my life.
Justice with favor have I always done;
Pray'rs and tears have moved me, gifts could never. 70
When have I aught exacted at your hands
But to maintain the King, the realm, and you?
Large gifts have I bestowed on learned clerks,
Because my book preferred me to the King;

80. **behoof:** benefit.

83. **reaching hands:** i.e., agents far afield to act for them.

88. **for:** because of; **watching:** remaining sleepless.

94. **caudle:** a hot drink, sometimes thickened with gruel, fed to sick people; a comfort. A **hempen caudle** is the remedy of being hanged.

95. **hatchet:** suggested by the title of a controversial tract attributed to John Lyly, *Pap with an Hatchet* (1589).

102. **affected:** sought.

And, seeing ignorance is the curse of God,   75
Knowledge the wing wherewith we fly to Heaven,
Unless you be possessed with devilish spirits,
You cannot but forbear to murder me.
This tongue hath parleyed unto foreign kings
For your behoof.   80

   Cade. Tut, when struckst thou one blow in the
field?

   Say. Great men have reaching hands: oft have I
    struck

Those that I never saw and struck them dead.   85

   Bevis. Oh, monstrous coward! what, to come behind folks?

   Say. These cheeks are pale for watching for your
    good.

   Cade. Give him a box o' the ear and that will make   90
'em red again.

   Say. Long sitting to determine poor men's causes
Hath made me full of sickness and diseases.

   Cade. Ye shall have a hempen caudle then and the
help of hatchet.   95

   Dick. Why dost thou quiver, man?

   Say. The palsy, and not fear, provokes me.

   Cade. Nay, he nods at us, as who should say, I'll be
even with you. I'll see if his head will stand steadier
on a pole, or no. Take him away and behead him.   100

   Say. Tell me wherein have I offended most?
Have I affected wealth or honor? Speak.
Are my chests filled up with extorted gold?
Is my apparel sumptuous to behold?
Whom have I injured, that ye seek my death?   105

109. **remorse:** compassion.

110. **and:** if.

112. **familiar:** demon; **o':** in.

128. **in capite:** "in chief," in feudal law signifying that a tenant held land directly from the King and paid perpetual rent for it. In effect, he had the use of the property but was not absolute owner. There is a pun on **maidenhead** and **capite** ("head").

129. **free:** licentious; free with their favors to him personally.

134. **brave:** splendid; hurrah.

These hands are free from guiltless bloodshedding,
This breast from harboring foul deceitful thoughts.
Oh, let me live!

   Cade. [*Aside*] I feel remorse in myself with his
words; but I'll bridle it: he shall die and it be but for 110
pleading so well for his life.—Away with him! he has
a familiar under his tongue: he speaks not o' God's
name. Go, take him away, I say, and strike off his
head presently; and then break into his son-in-law's
house, Sir James Cromer, and strike off his head, and 115
bring them both upon two poles hither.

   All. It shall be done.

   Say. Ah, countrymen! if when you make your
     prayers,
God should be so obdurate as yourselves,   120
How would it fare with your departed souls?
And therefore yet relent and save my life.

   Cade. Away with him! and do as I command ye.
                [*Exeunt some with Lord Say.*]
The proudest peer in the realm shall not wear a head
on his shoulders, unless he pay me tribute. There 125
shall not a maid be married but she shall pay to me
her maidenhead ere they have it. Men shall hold of
me *in capite;* and we charge and command that their
wives be as free as heart can wish or tongue can
tell.   130

   Dick. My lord, when shall we go to Cheapside and
take up commodities upon our bills?

   Cade. Marry, presently.

   All. Oh, brave!

[IV.viii.] Cade, about to order further death and destruction, meets Buckingham and Lord Clifford, who bring an ultimatum from the King offering free pardon to all who will abandon Cade and go home peaceably. His followers, already tired of him, agree to accept pardon and desert Cade, who takes to his heels, bitter at his men's faithlessness.

—————————————————

1. Fish Street: near London Bridge on the opposite side of the river from Southwark.

Enter one with the heads.

Cade. But is not this braver? Let them kiss one an- 135
other, for they loved well when they were alive. Now
part them again, lest they consult about the giving-up
of some more towns in France. Soldiers, defer the
spoil of the city until night: for, with these borne
before us, instead of maces, will we ride through the 140
streets; and at every corner have them kiss. Away!
                                                    Exeunt.

[Scene VIII. Southwark.]

*Alarum and retreat. Enter again Cade and all his
rabblement.*

Cade. Up Fish Street! Down St. Magnus' Corner!
Kill and knock down! Throw them into Thames!
(*Sound a parley.*) What noise is this I hear? Dare any
be so bold to sound retreat or parley when I command them kill?   5

Enter Buckingham and Old Clifford, [attended].

Buck. Ay, here they be that dare and will disturb
    thee:
Know, Cade, we come ambassadors from the King
Unto the commons whom thou hast misled,
And here pronounce free pardon to them all   10

22. **brave:** defiant.
28. **recreants:** cowards.

Henry V. From John Speed, *The Theatre of the Empire of Great Britain* (1627).

That will forsake thee and go home in peace.

  Cliff. What say ye, countrymen? Will ye relent
And yield to mercy whilst 'tis offered you;
Or let a rebel lead you to your deaths?
Who loves the King and will embrace his pardon,   15
Fling up his cap, and say, "God save His Majesty!"
Who hateth him and honors not his father,
Henry the Fifth, that made all France to quake,
Shake he his weapon at us and pass by.

  All. God save the King! God save the King!   20

  Cade. What, Buckingham and Clifford, are ye so
brave? And you, base peasants, do ye believe him?
Will you needs be hanged with your pardons about
your necks? Hath my sword therefore broke through
London gates, that you should leave me at the White   25
Hart in Southwark? I thought ye would never have
given out these arms till you had recovered your ancient freedom: but you are all recreants and dastards
and delight to live in slavery to the nobility. Let them
break your backs with burdens, take your houses over   30
your heads, ravish your wives and daughters before
your faces. For me, I will make shift for one; and so,
God's curse light upon you all!

  All. We'll follow Cade, we'll follow Cade!

  Cliff. Is Cade the son of Henry the Fifth,   35
That thus you do exclaim you'll go with him?
Will he conduct you through the heart of France
And make the meanest of you earls and dukes?
Alas, he hath no home, no place to fly to;
Nor knows he how to live but by the spoil,   40
Unless by robbing of your friends and us.

42. **at jar:** in contention; up in arms.
44. **make a start:** suddenly rise in revolt.
47. **Villiago:** actually Italian *vigliacco*, "coward."
48. **miscarry:** die.
53. **God on our side:** if God is on our side.
54. **A Clifford:** an identifying war cry, here signifying willingness to follow Clifford's lead.
60. **surprise:** capture.

Were't not a shame that, whilst you live at jar,
The fearful French, whom you late vanquished,
Should make a start o'er seas and vanquish you?
Methinks already in this civil broil   45
I see them lording it in London streets,
Crying "Villiago!" unto all they meet.
Better ten thousand baseborn Cades miscarry
Than you should stoop unto a Frenchman's mercy.
To France, to France, and get what you have lost;   50
Spare England, for it is your native coast.
Henry hath money, you are strong and manly;
God on our side, doubt not of victory.

  All. A Clifford! a Clifford! We'll follow the King and
Clifford.   55

  Cade. Was ever feather so lightly blown to and fro
as this multitude? The name of Henry the Fifth hales
them to an hundred mischiefs and makes them leave
me desolate. I see them lay their heads together to
surprise me. My sword make way for me, for here is   60
no staying. In despite of the devils and hell, have
through the very midst of you! And Heavens and
honor be witness that no want of resolution in me but
only my followers' base and ignominious treasons
makes me betake me to my heels.   *Exit.*   65

  Buck. What, is he fled? Go some and follow him;
And he that brings his head unto the King
Shall have a thousand crowns for his reward.
                          Exeunt some of them.
Follow me, soldiers: we'll devise a mean
To reconcile you all unto the King.   70
                                  Exeunt.

[IV.ix.] Buckingham and Lord Clifford bring the
repentant rebels to the King at Kenilworth, whence
they are dismissed to their homes with full pardons.
News comes that York has returned from Ireland
with an army, determined to remove Somerset from
the King's side.

1. **joyed:** enjoyed.
Ent. 10. **halters:** nooses.
15. **entertain:** receive.

[Scene IX. Kenilworth Castle.]

Sound trumpets. Enter King, Queen, and Somerset,
on the terrace.

  King. Was ever king that joyed an earthly throne
And could command no more content than I?
No sooner was I crept out of my cradle
But I was made a king, at nine months old.
Was never subject longed to be a king   5
As I do long and wish to be a subject.

    Enter Buckingham and [Old] Clifford.

  Buck. Health and glad tidings to your Majesty!
  King. Why, Buckingham, is the traitor Cade sur-
    prised?
Or is he but retired to make him strong?   10

Enter, [below,] multitudes, with halters about their
necks.

  Cliff. He is fled, my lord, and all his powers do yield
And humbly thus, with halters on their necks,
Expect your Highness' doom, of life or death.
  King. Then, Heaven, set ope thy everlasting gates,
To entertain my vows of thanks and praise!   15
Soldiers, this day have you redeemed your lives

23. **several:** respective; **countries:** abodes; neighborhoods.

25. **advertised:** informed.

28. **galloglasses:** mercenary soldiers more formidable, because more heavily armed, than kerns.

30. **still:** always.

36. **calmed:** becalmed; **with:** by.

37. **But:** even; just.

38. **second:** support.

Irish galloglasses and kern. From John Derricke, *The Image of Ireland* (1581; 1883 reprint).

And showed how well you love your prince and
    country.
Continue still in this so good a mind,
And Henry, though he be infortunate,   20
Assure yourselves, will never be unkind:
And so, with thanks and pardon to you all,
I do dismiss you to your several countries.
   All. God save the King! God save the King!

Enter a Messenger.

   Mess. Please it your Grace to be advertised   25
The Duke of York is newly come from Ireland
And with a puissant and a mighty power
Of galloglasses and stout kerns
Is marching hitherward in proud array,
And still proclaimeth, as he comes along,   30
His arms are only to remove from thee
The Duke of Somerset, whom he terms a traitor.
   King. Thus stands my state, 'twixt Cade and York
    distressed;
Like to a ship that, having 'scaped a tempest,   35
Is straightway calmed and boarded with a pirate.
But now is Cade driven back, his men dispersed;
And now is York in arms to second him.
I pray thee, Buckingham, go and meet him,
And ask him what's the reason of these arms.   40
Tell him I'll send Duke Edmund to the Tower;
And, Somerset, we will commit thee thither,
Until his army be dismissed from him.
   Som. My lord,

48. **brook:** tolerate.

‚‚‚‚‚‚‚‚‚‚‚‚‚‚‚‚‚‚‚‚‚‚‚‚‚‚‚‚‚‚‚‚‚‚‚‚‚

[IV.x.] Cade, famished after days of hiding, enters the garden of a Kentish gentleman in search of food. When the owner, Alexander Iden, comes upon him, Cade attacks him and is killed. Since Cade identified himself before he died, Iden cuts off his head and takes it to the King.

‚‚‚‚‚‚‚‚‚‚‚‚‚‚‚‚‚‚‚‚‚‚‚‚‚‚‚‚‚‚

4. **is laid for me:** has been ambushed to trap me; a countrywide search has been organized.

8. **sallet:** salad.

11. **sallet:** kind of helmet.

12. **brown bill:** a long-handled weapon.

I'll yield myself to prison willingly,   45
Or unto death, to do my country good.
   King. In any case, be not too rough in terms;
For he is fierce and cannot brook hard language.
   Buck. I will, my lord; and doubt not so to deal
As all things shall redound unto your good.   50
   King. Come, wife, let's in and learn to govern
     better;
For yet may England curse my wretched reign.
                 Flourish. Exeunt.

[Scene X. Kent. Iden's garden.]

Enter Cade.

   Cade. Fie on ambitions! Fie on myself, that have a
sword and yet am ready to famish! These five days
have I hid me in these woods and durst not peep out,
for all the country is laid for me; but now am I so
hungry that if I might have a lease of my life for a   5
thousand years I could stay no longer. Wherefore, on
a brick wall have I climbed into this garden, to see if
I can eat grass or pick a sallet another while, which
is not amiss to cool a man's stomach this hot weather.
And I think this word "sallet" was born to do me   10
good: for many a time, but for a sallet, my brainpan
had been cleft with a brown bill; and many a time,
when I have been dry and bravely marching, it hath
served me instead of a quart pot to drink in; and
now the word "sallet" must serve me to feed on.   15

16. **turmoiled:** surrounded by activity; unquiet.

22. **Sufficeth that I have:** it sufficeth that what I have.

25. **for a stray:** as a tame animal without apparent owner; **fee simple:** estate owned absolutely.

28. **ostrich:** see cut below.

30. **companion:** fellow (contemptuous).

35. **brave:** challenge.

37. **broached:** spilled.

Ostrich eating iron. From Gabriele Simeoni, *Le sententiose imprese* (1560).

Enter Iden [with Servants behind].

Iden. Lord, who would live turmoiled in the court
And may enjoy such quiet walks as these?
This small inheritance my father left me
Contenteth me, and worth a monarchy.
I seek not to wax great by others' waning   20
Or gather wealth, I care not with what envy:
Sufficeth that I have maintains my state
And sends the poor well pleased from my gate.

Cade. Here's the lord of the soil come to seize me
for a stray, for entering his fee simple without leave.   25
Ah, villain, thou wilt betray me and get a thousand
crowns of the King by carrying my head to him: but
I'll make thee eat iron like an ostrich and swallow my
sword like a great pin, ere thou and I part.

Iden. Why, rude companion, whatsoe'er thou be,   30
I know thee not: why then should I betray thee?
Is't not enough to break into my garden,
And, like a thief, to come to rob my grounds,
Climbing my walls in spite of me the owner,
But thou wilt brave me with these saucy terms?   35

Cade. Brave thee! Ay, by the best blood that ever
was broached, and beard thee too. Look on me well:
I have eat no meat these five days; yet, come thou
and thy five men, and if I do not leave you all as dead
as a doornail, I pray God I may never eat grass more.   40

Iden. Nay, it shall ne'er be said, while England
        stands,
That Alexander Iden, an esquire of Kent,

44. **odds:** advantage.

53–4. **As for words, whose greatness answers words,/ Let this my sword report what speech forbears:** although words are appropriately answered by similar language, Iden disdains to talk in Cade's vein but will let his sword speak for him.

55. **complete:** perfect.

72. **emblaze:** emblazon; display.

Took odds to combat a poor famished man.
Oppose thy steadfast-gazing eyes to mine,   45
See if thou canst outface me with thy looks.
Set limb to limb, and thou art far the lesser;
Thy hand is but a finger to my fist,
Thy leg a stick compared with this truncheon.
My foot shall fight with all the strength thou hast;   50
And if mine arm be heaved in the air,
Thy grave is digged already in the earth.
As for words, whose greatness answers words,
Let this my sword report what speech forbears.

   Cade. By my valor, the most complete champion   55
that ever I heard! Steel, if thou turn the edge, or cut
not out the burly-boned clown in chines of beef ere
thou sleep in thy sheath, I beseech God on my knees
thou mayst be turned to hobnails.

                  Here they fight. [Cade falls.]

Oh, I am slain! Famine and no other hath slain me.   60
Let ten thousand devils come against me, and give me
but the ten meals I have lost, and I'd defy them all.
Wither, garden; and be henceforth a burying place
to all that do dwell in this house, because the un-
conquered soul of Cade is fled.   65

   Iden. Is't Cade that I have slain, that monstrous
     traitor?
Sword, I will hallow thee for this thy deed
And hang thee o'er my tomb when I am dead.
Ne'er shall this blood be wiped from thy point,   70
But thou shalt wear it as a herald's coat,
To emblaze the honor that thy master got.

   Cade. Iden, farewell, and be proud of thy victory.

84. ungracious: wicked.

Tell Kent from me, she hath lost her best man, and
exhort all the world to be cowards; for I, that never   75
feared any, am vanquished by famine, not by valor.

Dies.

 Iden. How much thou wrongst me, Heaven be my
  judge.
Die, damned wretch, the curse of her that bare thee;
And as I thrust thy body in with my sword,   80
So wish I, I might thrust thy soul to hell.
Hence will I drag thee headlong by the heels
Unto a dunghill, which shall be thy grave,
And there cut off thy most ungracious head;
Which I will bear in triumph to the King,   85
Leaving thy trunk for crows to feed upon.

Exeunt, [Iden dragging out the body].

THE SECOND PART
OF
HENRY THE SIXTH

ACT V

[**V.i.**] Buckingham encounters York and in the King's name demands the reason for his return in arms. York claims that he comes with an army only to remove Somerset forcibly from the royal presence. When Buckingham states that Somerset is in the Tower, York yields. Iden enters with Cade's head and is knighted by the King and taken into his service. At this moment, the Queen enters with Somerset. York, in a rage, declares that King Henry is not fit to rule and must give way for one whom Heaven has ordained as sovereign—namely, himself. Somerset attempts to arrest York, who calls for his two sons to be his surety. York orders Lord Clifford to pay him homage as his rightful king, which Clifford refuses. Warwick and Salisbury declare their allegiance to York. The two factions defy each other and prepare for battle.

━━━━━━━━━━━━━━━━━━━━

6. **sancta majestas:** sacred majesty.

10. **it:** his hand.

12. **fleur-de-luce:** fleur-de-lis, emblem of French royalty.

[ACT V]

[Scene I. Fields between Dartford and Blackheath.]

*Enter York and his army of Irish, with Drum
and Colors.*

York. From Ireland thus comes York to claim his
    right
And pluck the crown from feeble Henry's head.
Ring, bells, aloud; burn, bonfires, clear and bright,
To entertain great England's lawful King.   5
Ah! *sancta majestas,* who would not buy thee dear?
Let them obey that knows not how to rule:
This hand was made to handle nought but gold.
I cannot give due action to my words
Except a sword or scepter balance it.   10
A scepter shall it have, have I a soul,
On which I'll toss the fleur-de-luce of France.

Enter Buckingham.

Whom have we here? Buckingham, to disturb me?
The King hath sent him, sure: I must dissemble.
    Buck. York, if thou meanest well, I greet thee well.   15

29. Ajax Telamonius: Ajax, son of Telamon, the Greek hero who ran mad when the arms of the dead Achilles were given to Ulysses instead of to him; he slew a herd of sheep, believing they were his enemies.

33. make fair weather: be pleasant; smile.

York. Humphrey of Buckingham, I accept thy
    greeting.
Art thou a messenger, or come of pleasure?

Buck. A messenger from Henry, our dread liege,
To know the reason of these arms in peace;   20
Or why thou, being a subject as I am,
Against thy oath and true allegiance sworn,
Should raise so great a power without his leave
Or dare to bring thy force so near the court.

York. [*Aside*] Scarce can I speak, my choler is so   25
    great!
Oh, I could hew up rocks and fight with flint,
I am so angry at these abject terms;
And now, like Ajax Telamonius,
On sheep or oxen could I spend my fury.   30
I am far better born than is the King,
More like a king, more kingly in my thoughts:
But I must make fair weather yet a while,
Till Henry be more weak and I more strong.—
Buckingham, I prithee, pardon me,   35
That I have given no answer all this while;
My mind was troubled with deep melancholy.
The cause why I have brought this army hither
Is to remove proud Somerset from the King,
Seditious to His Grace and to the state.   40

Buck. That is too much presumption on thy part:
But if thy arms be to no other end,
The King hath yielded unto thy demand:
The Duke of Somerset is in the Tower.

York. Upon thine honor, is he prisoner?   45
Buck. Upon mine honor, he is prisoner.

49. **St. George's field:** a field adjoining the parish church of St. George in Southwark.

63. **intends:** means.

67. **discomfited:** defeated.

York. Then, Buckingham, I do dismiss my pow'rs.
Soldiers, I thank you all: disperse yourselves.
Meet me tomorrow in St. George's field,
You shall have pay and everything you wish.   50
And let my sovereign, virtuous Henry,
Command my eldest son, nay, all my sons,
As pledges of my fealty and love.
I'll send them all as willing as I live:
Lands, goods, horse, armor, anything I have,   55
Is his to use, so Somerset may die.
    Buck. York, I commend this kind submission.
We twain will go into His Highness' tent.

Enter King and Attendants.

    King. Buckingham, doth York intend no harm to us,
That thus he marcheth with thee arm in arm?   60
    York. In all submission and humility
York doth present himself unto your Highness.
    King. Then what intends these forces thou dost
        bring?
    York. To heave the traitor Somerset from hence,   65
And fight against that monstrous rebel Cade,
Who since I heard to be discomfited.

Enter Iden, with Cade's head.

    Iden. If one so rude and of so mean condition
May pass into the presence of a king,
Lo, I present your Grace a traitor's head,   70
The head of Cade, whom I in combat slew.

77. an't like: if it please.

   King. The head of Cade! Great God, how just art
     Thou!
Oh, let me view his visage, being dead,
That living wrought me such exceeding trouble.   75
Tell me, my friend, art thou the man that slew him?
   Iden. I was, an't like your Majesty.
   King. How art thou called? and what is thy degree?
   Iden. Alexander Iden, that's my name;
A poor esquire of Kent, that loves his king.   80
   Buck. So please it you, my lord, 'twere not amiss
He were created knight for his good service.
   King. Iden, kneel down. [*He kneels.*] Rise up a
    knight.
We give thee for reward a thousand marks   85
And will that thou henceforth attend on us.
   Iden. May Iden live to merit such a bounty,
And never live but true unto his liege!   [*Rises.*]

Enter Queen and Somerset.

   King. See, Buckingham, Somerset comes with the
    Queen: 90
Go, bid her hide him quickly from the Duke.
   Queen. For thousand Yorks he shall not hide his
    head,
But boldly stand and front him to his face.
   York. How now! is Somerset at liberty?   95
Then, York, unloose thy long-imprisoned thoughts
And let thy tongue be equal with thy heart.
Shall I endure the sight of Somerset?
False King! why hast thou broken faith with me,

100. **abuse:** deceit.

105. **palmer:** religious pilgrim.

106. **awful:** awe-inspiring.

108–9. **Achilles' spear,/ Is able . . . to kill and cure:** classical writers reported that rust from Achilles' spear cured a wound that it had made. The meaning of the passage is the same as the proverb "Seek your salve where you got your sore."

121. **ward:** prison.

123. **amain:** with all speed.

125. **surety:** security; hostages.

Knowing how hardly I can brook abuse?   100
King did I call thee? No, thou art not King,
Not fit to govern and rule multitudes,
Which darest not, no, nor canst not, rule a traitor.
That head of thine doth not become a crown;
Thy hand is made to grasp a palmer's staff,   105
And not to grace an awful princely scepter.
That gold must round engirt these brows of mine,
Whose smile and frown, like to Achilles' spear,
Is able with the change to kill and cure.
Here is a hand to hold a scepter up,   110
And with the same to act controlling laws.
Give place: by Heaven, thou shalt rule no more
O'er him whom Heaven created for thy ruler.
   Som. O monstrous traitor! I arrest thee, York,
Of capital treason 'gainst the King and crown.   115
Obey, audacious traitor: kneel for grace.
   York. Wouldst have me kneel? First let me ask of
     these
If they can brook I bow a knee to man.
Sirrah, call in my sons to be my bail: [*Exit Attendant.*]   120
I know, ere they will have me go to ward,
They'll pawn their swords for my enfranchisement.
   Queen. Call hither Clifford: bid him come amain,
To say if that the bastard boys of York
Shall be the surety for their traitor father.   125
                  [*Exit Buckingham.*]
   York. O blood-bespotted Neapolitan,
Outcast of Naples, England's bloody scourge!
The sons of York, thy betters in their birth,

129. **bane:** destruction.

Shall be their father's bail; and bane to those
That for my surety will refuse the boys!   130

Enter Edward and Richard.

See where they come: I'll warrant they'll make it good.

Enter Clifford [and his Son].

Queen. And here comes Clifford to deny their bail.
Cliff. Health and all happiness to my lord the King!
                                    [Kneels.]
York. I thank thee, Clifford. Say, what news with   135
    thee?
Nay, do not fright us with an angry look.
We are thy sovereign, Clifford, kneel again:
For thy mistaking so, we pardon thee.
Cliff. This is my king, York, I do not mistake;   140
But thou mistakes me much to think I do.
To Bedlam with him! Is the man grown mad?
King. Ay, Clifford; a bedlam and ambitious humor
Makes him oppose himself against his king.
Cliff. He is a traitor: let him to the Tower,   145
And chop away that factious pate of his.
Queen. He is arrested but will not obey:
His sons, he says, shall give their words for him.
York. Will you not, sons?
Ed. Ay, noble father, if our words will serve.   150
Rich. And if words will not, then our weapons
    shall.

158. **astonish:** terrify; **fell-lurking:** lurking with deadly intent.

166. **suffered:** wounded.

170. **indigested lump:** referring to his hunchbacked body and to the belief that bear cubs were shapeless masses at birth that had to be licked into shape by their mothers.

Licking a bear cub into shape. From Guillaume de La Perrière, *Le théâtre des bon engins* (1539).

Cliff. Why, what a brood of traitors have we here!
York. Look in a glass and call thy image so:
I am thy king, and thou a false-heart traitor.   155
Call hither to the stake my two brave bears,
That with the very shaking of their chains
They may astonish these fell-lurking curs.
Bid Salisbury and Warwick come to me.
                         [*Exit Attendant.*]

     Enter the Earls of Warwick and Salisbury.

Cliff. Are these thy bears? We'll bait thy bears to   160
    death,
And manacle the bearward in their chains,
If thou darest bring them to the baiting place.
Rich. Oft have I seen a hot o'erweening cur
Run back and bite, because he was withheld;   165
Who, being suffered with the bear's fell paw,
Hath clapped his tail between his legs and cried:
And such a piece of service will you do,
If you oppose yourselves to match Lord Warwick.
Cliff. Hence, heap of wrath, foul indigested lump,   170
As crooked in thy manners as thy shape!
York. Nay, we shall heat you thoroughly anon.
Cliff. Take heed, lest by your heat you burn your-
    selves.
King. Why, Warwick, hath thy knee forgot to bow? 175
Old Salisbury, shame to thy silver hair,
Thou mad misleader of thy brainsick son!
What wilt thou on thy deathbed play the ruffian
And seek for sorrow with thy spectacles?

188. **That:** who, referring to Salisbury; **mickle:** much.

195. **dispense with:** arrange terms with.

202. **reave:** rob.

206. **sophister:** one skilled at framing false excuses.

209. **dignity:** honor; high position.

Oh, where is faith? Oh, where is loyalty?   180
If it be banished from the frosty head,
Where shall it find a harbor in the earth?
Wilt thou go dig a grave to find out war,
And shame thine honorable age with blood?
Why art thou old, and wantst experience?   185
Or wherefore dost abuse it, if thou hast it?
For shame! in duty bend thy knee to me,
That bows unto the grave with mickle age.
   Sal. My lord, I have considered with myself
The title of this most renowned duke   190
And in my conscience do repute His Grace
The rightful heir to England's royal seat.
   King. Hast thou not sworn allegiance unto me?
   Sal. I have.
   King. Canst thou dispense with Heaven for such an   195
    oath?
   Sal. It is great sin to swear unto a sin,
But greater sin to keep a sinful oath.
Who can be bound by any solemn vow
To do a murd'rous deed, to rob a man,   200
To force a spotless virgin's chastity,
To reave the orphan of his patrimony,
To wring the widow from her customed right,
And have no other reason for this wrong
But that he was bound by a solemn oath?   205
   Queen. A subtle traitor needs no sophister.
   King. Call Buckingham and bid him arm himself.
   York. Call Buckingham and all the friends thou hast;
I am resolved for death or dignity.
   Cliff. The first I warrant thee, if dreams prove true. 210

215. **burgonet:** steel helmet.

216. **know:** i.e., recognize (under battle conditions).

230. **stigmatic:** deformity; deformed one.

The bear and ragged staff, within the motto of the Order of the Garter. From Arthur Golding's translation of Ovid, *Metamorphoses* (1567).

War. You were best to go to bed and dream again,
To keep thee from the tempest of the field.

Cliff. I am resolved to bear a greater storm
That any thou canst conjure up today;
And that I'll write upon thy burgonet,   215
Might I but know thee by thy household badge.

War. Now, by my father's badge, old Neville's crest,
The rampant bear chained to the ragged staff,
This day I'll wear aloft my burgonet,
As on a mountain top the cedar shows   220
That keeps his leaves in spite of any storm,
Even to affright thee with the view thereof.

Cliff. And from thy burgonet I'll rend thy bear,
And tread it under foot with all contempt,
Despite the bearward that protects the bear.   225

Young Cliff. And so to arms, victorious father,
To quell the rebels and their complices.

Rich. Fie! charity, for shame! Speak not in spite,
For you shall sup with Jesu Christ tonight.

Young Cliff. Foul stigmatic, that's more than thou 230
    canst tell.

Rich. If not in Heaven, you'll surely sup in hell.

                        Exeunt [severally].

[V.ii.] At St. Albans the forces of York and the King meet in the first engagement of the Wars of the Roses. York kills Clifford, whose body is retrieved by his son. Young Clifford, noting that York does not spare old men whose fighting days should be past, vows that he will not spare even the babes of the enemy side. York's youngest son, Richard, kills Somerset in front of an alehouse called the Castle, thus fulfilling another of the prophecies. York's forces win, and the Queen Margaret urges the King to fly to London.

▬▬▬▬▬▬▬▬▬▬▬▬▬▬

4. **dead men's cries do fill the empty air:** i.e., the cries of dying men still hang in the air.

15. **chase:** quarry.

[Scene II. St. Albans.]

[*Alarums to the battle.*] *Enter Warwick.*

War. Clifford of Cumberland, 'tis Warwick calls:
And if thou dost not hide thee from the bear,
Now, when the angry trumpet sounds alarum,
And dead men's cries do fill the empty air,
Clifford, I say, come forth and fight with me.
Proud northern lord, Clifford of Cumberland,
Warwick is hoarse with calling thee to arms.

Enter York.

How now, my noble lord! What, all afoot?
   York. The deadly-handed Clifford slew my steed,
But match to match I have encountered him   1
And made a prey for carrion kites and crows
Even of the bonny beast he loved so well.

Enter [Old] Clifford.

   War. Of one or both of us the time is come.
   York. Hold, Warwick, seek thee out some other
      chase,   18
For I myself must hunt this deer to death.
   War. Then, nobly, York; 'tis for a crown thou fightst.
As I intend, Clifford, to thrive today,
It grieves my soul to leave thee unassailed.   *Exit.*

23. **fast:** firmly; irrevocably.

30. **lay:** stake; **Address:** prepare.

31. **La fin couronne les oeuvres:** "the end crowns the work," proverbial.

38. **minister:** agent.

46. **premised:** preordained.

Cliff. What seest thou in me, York? Why dost thou 2
    pause?

York. With thy brave bearing should I be in love,
But that thou art so fast mine enemy.

Cliff. Nor should thy prowess want praise and
    esteem   2
But that 'tis shown ignobly and in treason.

York. So let it help me now against thy sword
As I in justice and true right express it.

Cliff. My soul and body on the action both!

York. A dreadful lay! Address thee instantly.   3
                    [*They fight, and Clifford falls.*]

Cliff. La fin couronne les oeuvres.   [*Dies.*]

York. Thus war hath given thee peace, for thou art
    still.
Peace with his soul, Heaven, if it be thy will!   [*Exit.*]

Enter Young Clifford.

Young Cliff. Shame and confusion! all is on the rout; 3
Fear frames disorder, and disorder wounds
Where it should guard. O war, thou son of hell,
Whom angry Heavens do make their minister,
Throw in the frozen bosoms of our part
Hot coals of vengeance! Let no soldier fly.   4
He that is truly dedicate to war
Hath no self-love, nor he that loves himself
Hath not essentially but by circumstance
The name of valor. [*Seeing his dead father*] Oh, let
    the vile world end,   4
And the premised flames of the last day

49. **Particularities:** things pertaining to private persons; private things.

50. **cease:** quiet.

52. **livery:** garb; **advised:** judicious.

53. **reverence:** state of honored old age; **chair days:** days of aged infirmity.

59. **reclaims:** tames.

64. **Absyrtus:** brother of Medea, who delayed pursuit by killing him and throwing pieces of his body along her route when fleeing from her father with Jason and the Golden Fleece.

67. **Anchises:** father of Aeneas, who bore him from the burning city of Troy on his shoulders.

72. **paltry:** contemptible.

Medea, Jason, and the Golden Fleece. From Ovid, *Metamorphoses* (1565).

Knit earth and heaven together!
Now let the general trumpet blow his blast,
Particularities and petty sounds
To cease! Wast thou ordained, dear father,   5
To lose thy youth in peace, and to achieve
The silver livery of advised age,
And, in thy reverence and thy chair days, thus
To die in ruffian battle? Even at this sight
My heart is turned to stone: and while 'tis mine,   55
It shall be stony. York not our old men spares;
No more will I their babes: tears virginal
Shall be to me even as the dew to fire,
And beauty that the tyrant oft reclaims
Shall to my flaming wrath be oil and flax.   60
Henceforth I will not have to do with pity:
Meet I an infant of the house of York,
Into as many gobbets will I cut it
As wild Medea young Absyrtus did.
In cruelty will I seek out my fame.   65
Come, thou new ruin of old Clifford's house:
As did Aeneas old Anchises bear,
So bear I thee upon my manly shoulders;
But then Aeneas bare a living load,
Nothing so heavy as these woes of mine.   70

> [*Exit, bearing off his father.*]

Enter Richard and Somerset to fight. [Somerset is killed.]

Rich. So, lie thou there;
For underneath an alehouse' paltry sign,

74. **the wizard:** referring to the spirit's answer to Bolingbroke's question as to Somerset's fate (I. [iv.] 36–9).

75. **hold thy temper:** keep thy resilient hardness.

84. **give the enemy way:** give way before the enemy; **secure:** safeguard; save.

85. **can no more but fly:** can do nothing but fly.

95. **discomfit:** defeat.

96. **parts:** partisans; followers.

The Castle in St. Albans, Somerset
Hath made the wizard famous in his death.
Sword, hold thy temper; heart, be wrathful still: 75
Priests pray for enemies, but princes kill. *[Exit.]*

Fight. Excursions. Enter King, Queen, and others.

Queen. Away, my lord! You are slow: for shame,
 away!
King. Can we outrun the Heavens? Good Margaret,
 stay. 80
Queen. What are you made of? You'll nor fight nor
 fly:
Now is it manhood, wisdom, and defense,
To give the enemy way, and to secure us
By what we can, which can no more but fly. 85
      Alarum afar off.
If you be ta'en, we then should see the bottom
Of all our fortunes: but if we haply scape,
As well we may, if not through your neglect,
We shall to London get, where you are loved,
And where this breach now in our fortunes made 90
May readily be stopped.

Enter [Young] Clifford.

Young Cliff. But that my heart's on future mischief
 set,
I would speak blasphemy ere bid you fly:
But fly you must. Uncurable discomfit 95
Reigns in the hearts of all our present parts.

98. their day and them our fortune give: i.e., such a victory as they now have, while they endure our present ill fortune.

▬▬▬▬▬▬▬▬▬▬▬▬▬▬▬▬▬

[V.iii.] York and his followers congratulate themselves on the victory, although it is not perfect, since the King and Queen have escaped. York suggests that they follow the King's party to London before the King can convene a Parliament.

▬▬▬▬▬▬▬▬▬▬▬▬▬▬▬▬▬

3. brush: onslaught; hostile attack.

4. brow: height; prime.

5. occasion: opportunity.

9. holp: helped.

10. bestrid him: straddled his prostrate body and fought off attackers.

Away, for your relief! and we will live
To see their day and them our fortune give.
Away, my lord, away!

Exeunt.

[Scene III. Fields near St. Albans.]

Alarum. Retreat. Enter York, Richard, Warwick, and
Soldiers, with Drum and Colors.

  York. Of Salisbury, who can report of him,
That winter lion, who in rage forgets
Aged contusions and all brush of time,
And, like a gallant in the brow of youth,
Repairs him with occasion? This happy day   5
Is not itself, nor have we won one foot,
If Salisbury be lost.
  Rich.   My noble father,
Three times today I holp him to his horse,
Three times bestrid him: thrice I led him off,   10
Persuaded him from any further act.
But still where danger was, still there I met him;
And like rich hangings in a homely house,
So was his will in his old feeble body.
But, noble as he is, look where he comes.   15

Enter Salisbury.

  Sal. Now, by my sword, well hast thou fought
    today:

22. have not got that which we have: i.e., we have the victory but it is inconclusive, since the King and Queen have escaped.

24. opposites: enemies.

27. present: immediate.

By the mass, so did we all. I thank you, Richard.
God knows how long it is I have to live;
And it hath pleased Him that three times today   20
You have defended me from imminent death.
Well, lords, we have not got that which we have:
'Tis not enough our foes are this time fled,
Being opposites of such repairing nature.

   York. I know our safety is to follow them;   25
For, as I hear, the King is fled to London,
To call a present court of Parliament.
Let us pursue him ere the writs go forth.
What says Lord Warwick? Shall we after them?

   War. After them! nay, before them, if we can.   30
Now, by my faith, lords, 'twas a glorious day.
St. Albans' battle won by famous York
Shall be eternized in all age to come.
Sound drum and trumpets, and to London all:
And more such days as these to us befall!   35

Exeunt.

Could I come near your beauty with my nails,
I'd set my Ten Commandments in your face.
[*Duchess*—I.iii.141–42]

When such strings jar, what hope of harmony?
[*King*—II.i.72]

Thus sometimes hath the brightest day a cloud;
And after summer evermore succeeds
Barren winter, with his wrathful, nipping cold:
So cares and joys abound, as seasons fleet.
[*Gloucester*—II.iv.1–5]

Smooth runs the water where the brook is deep.
[*Suffolk*—III.i.53]

Thrice is he armed that hath his quarrel just,
And he but naked, though locked up in steel,
Whose conscience with injustice is corrupted.
[*King*—III.ii.246–48]

I thank them for their tender loving care.
[*King*—III.ii.297]

The gaudy, blabbing, and remorseful day
Is crept into the bosom of the sea.
[*Lieutenant*—IV.i.1–2]

It was never merry world in England since
gentlemen came up.   [*Holland*—IV.ii.8–9]

I will make it felony to drink small beer.
[*Cade*—IV.ii.66–7]

The first thing we do, let's kill all the lawyers.
[*Dick*—IV.ii.75]

It will be proved to thy face that thou hast men
about thee that usually talk of a noun and a
verb and such abominable words as no Christian
ear can endure to hear.   [*Cade*—IV.vii.38–41]

Ignorance is the curse of God,
Knowledge the wing wherewith we fly to Heaven.
[*Say*—IV.vii.75–6]

I'll make thee eat iron like an ostrich.   [*Cade*—IV.x.28]

As dead as a doornail.   [*Cade*—IV.x.39–40]

Washington Square Press Relaunches
the **Enriched Classics Series** with Each
New Edition Featuring Expanded and Updated
Reader's Supplements

ADVENTURES OF HUCKLEBERRY FINN
Mark Twain. . . . . 88803-X/$4.99

THE GOOD EARTH
Pearl S. Buck. . . . . 51012-6/$6.99

LAME DEER, SEEKER OF VISIONS
John (Fire) Lame Deer & Erdoes. . . . 88802-1/$5.50

MY ANTONIA
Willa Cather. . . . . 89086-7/$5.50

OEDIPUS THE KING
Sophocles. . . . . 88804-8/$5.50

THE SCARLET LETTER
Nathaniel Hawthorne. . . . . 51011-8/$4.99

DR. JEKYLL AND MR. HYDE
Robert Louis Stevenson. . . . . 53210-3/$3.99

FRANKENSTEIN
Mary Shelley. . . . . .53150-6/$4.99

THE RED BADGE OF COURAGE
Stephen Crane. . . . . .00275-9/$5.99

A TALE OF TWO CITIES
Charles Dickens. . . . . .00274-0/$5.99

A CHRISTMAS CAROL
Charles Dickens. . . . . .47369-7/$3.99

WSP